'The Hong Kong Brief'

A novel by

Neal Hardin

ISBN 9798668405244

For you, the readers of books.

Acknowledgement

With thanks to my friend, Leo Batt

for his advice, guidance and suggestions.

Chapter 1

London, April 2017

The melodic sound of the busker's guitar echoed against the low, tiled ceiling of the pedestrian walkway. The artist was serenading the swarm of commuters buzzing through the cross tunnels in Oxford Circus tube station. She sang… '*But February made me shiver…With every paper I'd deliver…Bad news on the doorstep…'*

Dave Moseley, his head down, his thoughts elsewhere, didn't register that she was singing the second stanza of 'Bye-Bye Miss American Pie' which just happened to be one of his favourite pieces of music. She had arranged it in a jaunty tempo that sounded more up-beat than the Don McLean original. But the words still recalled the memories of years gone and the tragic death of Buddy Holly and his music.

Moseley was aiming for the strip of light at the top of the stairs and some much-needed fresh air after the stale tainted humidity on the underground train.

As he emerged into the opening at the summit he drew in a breath. The sharp, cold, icy breeze whipping along Regent Street caught him by surprise. He let out an audible 'brrrr', then shivered as the chill hit his senses. In response, he pulled the collar of his coat up and hunched his shoulders like a man who was about to be drenched by a bucketful of cold water. Despite the watery sunshine, London was still in the grip of the back end of a week-long cold snap that had left the early April days feeling more like the first week of

January. The pavement was slippery under foot. He slipped his hands into the deep recess of the coat pockets and made a tight fist. The sounds of the city clamped around him and gave him an increased jolt of energy. After all, he was in the centre of one of the world's truly great cities, for this part of central London, situated right in the middle of the bustling West End, was a busy backdrop of people going about their business.

He walked along Regent Street for a couple of hundred yards then took a left and ventured into a maze of narrow, tight thoroughfares that marked the beginning of Soho. An area full of eateries, hotspot pubs, small niche shops and the home of many micro-businesses.

His office wasn't too far away. Once he was inside and he had a cup of hot, steaming coffee in his hands he would feel much better and warmer.

Dave Moseley was a proverbial one-man band. He had been in the private investigator business for two years short of a decade. His office was in a cramped, two-room space on the first floor of a building above a pastry shop on Broadwick Street. He wasn't exactly the Sam Spade or the Philip Marlowe of London town. His list of cases didn't consist of assignments in which he had to use his wit and charm to get out of sticky situations, neither were they glamorous or demanding. His work load usually concerned the surveillance of errant company employees or a suspicious husband wanting to keep tabs on his wife who he suspected – mostly incorrectly – was involved with the local Casanova. The guy who couldn't keep his pecker in his pants. The private investigation business wasn't like that portrayed in the movies, in which some character who resembled a modern-day Humphrey Bogart was assigned to follow a stunning blonde to an exotic beach side location. Or on the other side of the coin, a criminal to some desolate former industrial site that was now a rust strung carcass of decay. Nor was he paid thousands of pounds to crack some high-end jewellery theft. His assignments tended to involve the more hum-drum things in life, that sadly, for him, didn't involve the former scenario. Still it paid okay and he had a reasonably good standard of living, though – for the record – being a private detective in modern day Britain wasn't all it was cracked up to be. It was a hard slog and he was in a dog-eat-dog kind of industry that involved things that in some cases were close to being unethical.

He made it to his office within five minutes of leaving the underground station. His priority was to fill the kettle, then turn on the heating and open the post. The office had a desk, a PC, and several metal cabinets full of files suspended on plastic runners. There were diplomas attached to the walls, a thin rug on the floor, dust on top of the cabinets and a lack of sumptuous decoration. The plaster walls were a shade of mint paint. As very few clients ever visited his office, he never had much need to worry about the look of the place. He preferred to conduct business by email or face-to-face meetings in mutually agreed locations, sometimes in full view of witnesses, other times in private.

Behind his desk was a window with a view onto the narrow width of the street below. On the wall were two glass frames, held there by an ample amount of blu-tack. One contained a photograph of Humphrey Bogart in his portrayal of Dashiell Hammett's alter-ego Sam Spade, the other was a photograph of Paul Newman as Ross MacDonald's private detective, Lew Harper. Moseley loved private-eye movies. His all-time favourite was one of the best movies ever made, Chinatown. He just loved the character Jake Gittes, played so wonderfully by Jack Nicholson.

As a former Met police detective, Dave Moseley knew the score and had the wherewithal to be good at what he did. He would confess that he didn't have a selection of one-liners and the laconic charisma of those aforementioned fictional characters. Still he knew the ins and outs of the game. He had divorced both his wife and the Met police at the age of thirty-eight. That was getting on for eight years now. At forty-six years of age he viewed life from a philosophical plateau of whatever-will-be-will-be. He dealt with everything modern day life could sling at him to eke out a decent existence. He resided in a small flat in a 1950s building on a stretch of Knightsbridge, therefore he was literally a couple of hundred yards from the beating heart of the city.

On this day, he was sitting at his desk for ten to ten, scanning through the pages of a morning red top newspaper, when he was distracted by the flashing, red light on the telephone on his desk.

He closed the newspaper, then pressed the loudspeaker button. "Dave Moseley Private Investigator," he said. "How can I help you today?" This was his normal opening patter for the question asked at the end invited the caller to indulge in shared conversation.

There was no instant reply, so he asked the question for a second time. He waited for an answer with his finger poised over the terminate button. He could just make out the sound of a breath on the other end of the line.

"Hello," came a hushed voice from down the line.

"Good morning. How can I help you today?" Moseley asked again.

"It is my daughter-in-law," came the reply in precisely worded English. Hearing the speaker's accent, for the first time, suggested that English wasn't the one he used for day-to-day communication.

"What about your daughter-in-law?" he asked.

"She is…" the caller paused in mid-sentence and seemed to lose the will to continue.

"She is what?"

"Missing."

The caller was hesitant. His accent sounded oriental, Chinese, or Korean or somewhere from that part of the world. Moseley reached for a pen and a notepad.

"What is the name of your daughter-in-law?" he asked.

"Lily Fung," he replied.

"Lily? L-I-L-Y? Fung? F-U-N-G?" Moseley asked.

"Yes."

"How long has she been missing?"

"Two to three weeks," came the reply.

The caller was definitely not a young man. There was a throaty edge to his voice which suggested he was in his late sixties or early seventies. Moseley saw the face of an elderly Chinese man appear in his mind's eye. Almond shape eyes, a yellow tint to his skin and short grey wiry hair.

"How old is Lily?" he asked as he scribbled the name, LILY FUNG onto the note-pad.

"Twenty-eight," came the reply.

"Do you want me to help you find your daughter-in-law?" Moseley asked.

"Yes. She leave home three weeks ago. Nobody see her since."

"Where's home?" Moseley asked.

"Kensington," came the reply. Moseley wrote: RICH and CHINESE on the notepad in upper case letters, next to the name of LILY FUNG. He was instantly intrigued.

"Do you know where she has gone?" he asked.

"Yes."

"Where?"

"Hong Kong," came the reply.

"Hong Kong!" Moseley asked seeking confirmation.

"Yes."

"Do you know where in Hong Kong?"

"I think so."

"What would you like me to do if I find her?" Moseley asked.

"Find her and bring her back to London," the caller said.

"What if she doesn't want to come back?"

"You tell her to come back," said the caller with a hint of command in the tone.

"Okay. Is she in Hong Kong with anyone?"

"Yes."

"Who?"

"The man who take her away from my son."

"A male friend?" Moseley asked cagily and warily.

"But she already married to my son. Hue."

"Why doesn't your son go to Hong Kong to ask her to come back?" Moseley asked.

"He can't," replied the caller.

Moseley was about to ask why his son couldn't go to Hong Kong to find his wife, but thought better of it. An image of a family in dispute or in some kind of marital crisis filled his mind. It was too early to jump to such a conclusion. Maybe there was a sound, legitimate reason why his son couldn't go to Hong Kong to bring his wife back to London. Did he have some connections to the troubles in that part of the world? Or was it for other reasons that weren't immediately obvious?

"Do you know her whereabouts in Hong Kong?" he asked.

"Yes."

"And you'd like me to go over there and persuade her, because that's all I can do, to come back?"

"Yes."

Moseley quickly summarised the task and considered his options. He refrained from asking the caller any more probing questions at this time.

"Okay," he said. "What I suggest is that we meet to discuss the brief face-to-face. Is that agreeable with you?" he asked.

"That is agree," the caller replied.

"If you require me to go to Hong Kong to find your daughter-in-law this is something I can do. Is that okay?" There was no immediate response to the question. "Would you like to meet with me to discuss the job?"

"Yes. That is acceptable to me," said the chap, breaking the word 'acceptable' into its four syllables.

"We can meet in my office or a place of your choice. It's completely up to you."

"You come to my home," said the caller.

"That's fine. Can I ask your name?" Moseley asked.

"My name is Ho Fung."

"Where is your home, Mr Fung?"

He provided Moseley with an address on a street in the heart of Belgravia. One of London's most desirable and expensive locations to live in. Dave Moseley was even more intrigued. He looked at the clock on the wall.

"What time would you like to meet?" he asked.

"Can you be here at two-thirty?"

"Today?"

"Yes."

"Yes. I can."

And with that Mr Fung terminated the conversation.

The time was ten-fifteen. A day that had started off quiet and cold was about to get a whole lot more interesting and a lot warmer.

Following the telephone conversation Moseley got straight on-line and carried out some desk research. He typed 'Ho Fung' into Wikipedia to see if it had anything on that name. After a couple of clicks of the mouse he had a good stash of information to hand. He was ultimately surprised by what he discovered. If it was the same person. A man by the name of Ho Fung, had been a major industrialist in Hong Kong in the engineering and the ship building industry during the seventies and the eighties. He had amassed quite a fortune. His business interests had links to large multinationals based in China and elsewhere throughout South-East Asia. In a rather grainy black and white photograph taken a few years before there was an image of Ho Fung. He had typical Chinese features, a short nose, narrow eyes, and a pallor shade to his skin. According to his Wiki page he had two children, a son called Hue and a daughter called Mia, aged forty and thirty-six, respectively. Was he the same man? At this time, he had no way of knowing.

If it was his daughter-in-law and he accepted the job there was absolutely no guarantee he would be able to find her in the teeming hustle and bustle of Hong Kong. If he did, would he be able to persuade her to return to London with him? After all, he assumed she had left her husband to take up with someone else under her own free will.

What Moseley later discovered through some more desk research was that Ho Fung had left Hong Kong in early 1997, three months before the Chinese takeover of the former British administrated territory. He brought his family and all his money to London, rather than take the journey to North America where many Hong Kong Chinese had headed before the handover and return to Chinese control. He and his family were now naturalised British citizens and European Union passport holders.

Chapter 2

The afternoon temperature was up a few degrees from the low of the morning chill. The sun was high in the sky and beginning to spread a vibrant orange glow over the streets of central London. Shadow from the row of buildings on the east side of Sloane Street was slowly progressing across the road like an incoming tide. Despite still being on the cool side it wasn't such a bad day for mid-April. The city wasn't yet swelled with tourists. As a result, Londoners could still get from A to B without too much hassle.

Moseley made his way into Belgravia and walked through the streets, with their pristine smartness and up-market *savoir-vivre.* The Fung residence was the last but one house in a long row that was situated in a cul-de-sac at the end of Seaton Place. At the top of the street was an opening that led into a small square which was encased by tall poplar trees set aside a grassy area. All the properties were high, five storey, white-walled stucco houses, behind wrought iron black metal railings that lined the street. Similar balconies ran along the entire length of the first floor in front of high, floor to ceiling windows. All had steps leading to solid front doors and steps going down to a basement level.

He stepped off the pavement, up a step, onto a tiled porch and approached the front door that was under the shade of the overhead balcony. He pressed a door bell in an intercom and waited for a response. A quick glance at his wrist told him he was dead on time.

Within a few seconds of pressing the bell, the front door opened and a small middle-aged lady with oriental features appeared. She was wearing a kind of grey housemaid's uniform. She had a somewhat glum, unwelcoming expression on her face. Looking beyond her shoulder he could see onto a vestibule with a shining, marble floor and blanch walls. A black-carpeted staircase on the right-hand side led up to the first floor. A corridor straight ahead went into the back of the house. A scent from lavender incense sticks filled his nostrils.

The lady in the maid's uniform observed him, still unsmiling, then she nodded her head at him.

"Mr David Moseley. Here to see Mr Fung," he said.

She didn't say a word, but opened the door wide and invited him inside with an inward wave of her hand. He stepped over the threshold, wiped his shoes on a thick brush door mat and entered the vestibule that was furnished with a Queen Anne style antique writing bureau and a matching chair. Both probably early nineteenth-century and French in origin. Several large, gold leaf traditional Chinese dragon statues were dotted here and there on the floor. A silk-thread embroidered picture of a young woman sitting on a tree branch playing a flute was attached to a wall. Close by was a Hong Kong British flag placed inside a gleaming glass case.

The maid came past him. "This way," she said in a faint voice. She led him into the hallway. He followed her for a few paces to an open door and she escorted him inside a formal reception room that faced the street. There was a curvy back sofa in a gold fabric covering and a single chair to a side. A multi-coloured rug covered the floor. A large mahogany desk with intricate carvings was placed by the back wall. Light was streaming in through a pair of narrow, high windows that were covered with open venetian blinds. The room was spotlessly clean and tidy.

The high ceiling had a central rose from where a cut-glass chandelier was hanging. An open fireplace and ornate tiled fire surround were the dominant features in the room. Above that was a gold and silver twine wallcovering of a Chinese landscape scene with rolling hills in the backdrop and a lake in the foreground.

She pointed to the sofa, but remained mute. Moseley nodded his head. He stepped to the sofa, plumped down, sat back and crossed his legs. She immediately backed out of the room to leave him alone and closed the door behind her. The Fung family were obviously very wealthy. Wealthier than the average Joe and far wealthier than the average Hong Kong Chinese family. Moseley adjusted his tie to make sure the knot was tight into the shirt collar.

Five minutes passed with no one coming to see him. It was as if they were waiting to see if he would become impatient and leave. Maybe they were testing him. Of course, he wouldn't leave until someone asked him to do so.

He was beginning to feel like the forgotten man when the door opened and a man stepped into the room. He was alone.

Moseley got to his feet and offered him his open hand. "Mr Fung?" he asked, assuming he was the client. The man gave him a solemn nod of his head. "Nice to meet you. My name is David

Moseley of Moseley Private Investigation services." It was the standard patter.

The man didn't smile. He was in his late sixties to early seventies and had the common oriental features. His head was lined with thick, short cropped wiry, grey hair. His skin had a pallid yellow tint. He had small liver spots around his eyes. He did resemble the man in the wiki photograph. He was a short chap, only about five feet two or three. Thin and gaunt. His waist wouldn't have measured more than thirty-two. But dignified looking. As you would expect for a wealthy individual.

Fung looked at Moseley then took his hand and they exchanged the briefest of handshakes. "Please be seated," he said. Moseley reassumed his place on the sofa. Ho Fung went to the desk and sat in a black leather armchair. Moseley noticed the liver spots on his face and how they were almost like for like down both sides of his cheeks. He had thin almond-shaped eyes behind loose lids.

He was wearing an everyday plain blue acrylic cardigan over a chequered shirt and grey trousers. The clasp of an expensive watch on his left wrist. He looked closely at Moseley.

"Thank you for come to see me today," he said in a heartfelt tone. His English was good, though not word perfect. Moseley nodded his head in a deferential manner. He wasn't going to say anything until he was asked a direct question.

"My daughter-in-law she go back to Hong Kong with her lover. I need someone to find her and bring her back here." Moseley didn't respond and let him continue. "She leave her husband, my son, and bring dishonour to my family."

Moseley uncrossed his legs. He was trying to assess Fung's integrity. He spoke in an even measured tone and hadn't displayed any residue anger. He appeared to be in full control of his emotions.

"She go with a play…boy. She fall for this man and leave her husband. Her husband, he is sad," he said. Moseley kept his expression neutral and continued to listen with his eyes. Fung continued. "You go to Hong Kong and bring her back here," he instructed.

Moseley considered his words for all of three seconds. "I'll have to see," he replied.

"What you need to see?" Fung asked. Perhaps he now realised this wasn't going to be as straight forward as it sounded.

"A few things," Moseley replied. He dipped a hand into a side coat pocket and extracted a notepad with a pen clipped to it. "Can I ask you a few questions?" he asked.

Fung thought about it for a moment, then nodded his head.

"What's your daughter-in-law's name?"

"Lily Fung."

"How old is Lily?"

"She twenty-eight."

"What's her background?" he asked. Fung seemed confused by the question. "Does she have any business interests?" Moseley asked.

"No."

"Do they have any children?"

"No."

"What's the name of the man she went with?"

"Leo Sinnott."

"Please can you spell that?"

Fung spelt out the name in clearly pronounced letters. "L-E-O…S-I-N-N-O-T-T."

Moseley wrote it down onto the notepad. "What's the name of your son?" he asked.

"Hue."

"Why doesn't Hue want to go to Hong Kong to find her and bring her back?"

"He not want to go to Hong Kong." He didn't offer any explanation as to why this was the case. Maybe there was a legitimate reason why he didn't want to or couldn't return to Hong Kong. Though he didn't seem to want to elaborate.

"Okay. Do you know where she is right now?" Moseley asked.

"He has a home in an apartment in the Leighton Hill area."

Moseley wrote it down on his pad. He had spent some time in Hong Kong ten years ago, and recalled the name of the area. "How did she meet…," he paused to look at his notepad. "Leo Sinnott?" he hoped he had pronounced it correctly.

"He come to London on business. He seduce Lily and persuade her to go back with him."

"How long was he here in the UK?" Moseley asked.

"Several weeks."

"What was he doing here? Do you know?"

"He is race horse trainer in Hong Kong. He visits some horse auction in England to buy racehorses for Hong Kong owners."

Moseley wrote, 'horse racing trainer' on the pad. "Did he target her from the outset?" he asked.

Fung seemed fazed by the question. "What you mean?" he asked.

Moseley had to think this through carefully and not put ideas into his head. "Do you think his intentions towards her were genuine?"

"I not know."

"Do you have the address?"

"Yes."

"And you think she could be there?"

"I think so."

"Why do you think so?"

"Because she told me."

"When did you last speak to her?"

"I not speak to her."

"How do you know where she is?" Moseley asked.

"Because she writes to me."

"And she gave you an address?"

"Yes, that right."

Moseley wasn't going to ask him why he wanted her back here. Maybe there was a good reason why she had left her husband, but this seemed to be of little interest to Fung. It could all be about family honour rather than anything untoward. “You go to Hong Kong to find her and bring her back?” Fung said in a raised tone. Again, expressing his desire that she had to return.

Moseley’s face displayed a neutral look. “I can go, but if I’m being truthful, I can’t guarantee that I can bring her back. I can’t force her to return,” he said.

“You try?”

“Yes. I can try.”

“Good. When can you go?”

Moseley had already checked the times of the flights leaving London for Hong Kong. “There are a few seats left on a flight from Heathrow tomorrow afternoon at two. I can be on that flight.”

Fung retained an impassive face. “Good,” he said. “Be on flight. Do you know anyone in Hong Kong?” he asked.

Moseley smiled. “I spent some time there about ten years ago.”

“Doing what?”

“I was there on police business for several weeks. We were seeking to extradite a British man back to the UK to stand trial,” Moseley said.

“Do you know anyone there?”

“I know a couple of people. A guy called Laurie Sullivan was a detective in the Hong Kong force. He showed me around the city. We worked together on the case and he was my interpreter.”

“Is he still there?”

"In Hong Kong?" Fung didn't reply. "Yes. As far as I know he's still lives in Kowloon. I still keep in contact with him from time to time. A card at Christmas. The occasional email. That kind of thing."

"This man. He might be useful to you?"

"Could be." Fung smiled at him for the first time. "Tell me about," Moseley looked at his notes. "Leo Sinnott."

"He is race horse trainer at Happy Valley. He also a gigolo," he snarled. "He uses women," he snarled once again. He clearly had a genuine dislike for the man who had taken his daughter-in-law from his son.

"Can you give me his address?"

Fung opened a drawer in the desk and extracted two sheets of paper. He placed them on the desk top, then slid them towards Moseley. He reached out of the seat to take them.

One was a folded piece of plain white paper from a pad; the other item was a glossy hardback photograph showing two people. A Chinese couple. He opened the folded paper and written there on the inside was an address in the Leighton Hill district of the city.

Fung sat back into the armchair and sighed out loud. It seemed as if a huge weight had been lifted from his shoulders. Moseley did wonder why he had asked him to take on the job and not rely on a Hong Kong operative to contact Lily Fung and persuade her to return to London. Perhaps he didn't trust anyone out there. It crossed his mind to ask Mr Fung, but he refrained from doing so. He looked at Fung. He admired his style and character. He was akin to a wise Chinese philosopher from a bygone age who displayed great wisdom and foresight.

"Can we talk about my fees?" Moseley asked. Fung nodded his head once. "I charge one thousand pounds a day, plus expenses, payable at the end of the job." Fung nodded his head once again. "One more question. Do you want me to contact you with progress?"

"No. I just want her back here. When she is back, I be happy man," Fung said.

Moseley pursed his lips then nodded his head. He looked at the photograph. It was of a couple who were standing slightly apart. Like a married couple, who maybe didn't want to remain married for much longer. The man was on the right of the shot, the woman on the left. It looked as if it had been taken at a social event of some description because it was an internal location and they were both dressed in evening wear. He was in a dark lounge suit. She was in a long, dark dress. She was taller than her husband. "I assume this is your son and his wife?" Moseley said.

"That is my son Hue and his wife Lily Fung," he replied.

She was an attractive woman with high cheek bones and a pretty face. Petite looking and very slim. She had long, straight black hair that reached the turn of her waist. She looked almost flat-chested as the slit in the dress revealed little in the way of cleavage. Hue Fung, her husband looked overweight and podgy. He wore thick black-framed spectacles over his eyes. His suit looked expensive Saville Row. Definitely not off the peg from some cheap Oxford Street store. It reeked of top end tailoring.

"When was this taken?" Moseley asked.

"Last year. At my seventy-fifth birthday party."

"May I keep it?"

"Yes, of course."

Moseley carefully slipped the photograph into his inside coat pocket, along with the paper with the address on it. His brief was simple, in the extreme, he had to find Lily Fung and return her to London.

"When you leave for Hong Kong?" Fung asked.

"Tomorrow afternoon on a British Airways flight."

Fung got to his feet. Moseley did likewise. Fung looked at him. "Thank you," he said.

He went to the closed door, opened it and led Moseley out into the vestibule, across the floor and on towards the front door. Light was beaming through a window to spread its reflection over the marble floor. The gold leaf of the big dragon statues glinted in the light. The housemaid appeared. She opened the front door to let him out.

Moseley was soon walking along the pavement and past the steps going down to a door leading into the basement. His first stop was a travel agent on Sloane Street. He would get himself a seat on the BA flight and pay for a room in a central hotel for five nights. If Fung was picking up the tab it would be a five-star hotel in the best part of Wanchai. That got him thinking about contacting Laurie Sullivan to tell him he was coming over to HK for a visit. Laurie Sullivan was a detective in the Hong Kong police force when the territory was under British control. He had stayed on following the handover in 1997 and remained in the HK police for a further twelve years or so until he retired in 2009. He still lived in Kowloon. Moseley had met him when he went to HK to extradite a commodities dealer wanted in London for fraud. Sullivan was fluent in Cantonese.

When Moseley came over Sullivan had shown him the ropes and the city. They got along fine. Although they hadn't met face-to-face for three years, when Sullivan came home for a short visit, Moseley still sent him an email now and again to ask him how he was getting on and enjoying his retirement. Although he was now in his mid-sixties, Sullivan was an active guy in that he kept fit and his ear close to everything that was going on. Moseley was more than pleased that he had kept in touch with him because he could be a big help. It was almost as if it was meant to be.

Chapter 3

The following day, Tuesday, Moseley made it onto the British Airways mid-afternoon flight to Hong Kong. He secured the last remaining seat in business class. He had paid for a room in a five-star hotel in the heart of the Wanchai district, the bustling epicentre of central Hong Kong island. He planned to stay for five nights.

He knew from his previous visit to Hong Kong that there are few places in this world to match the vibrancy and pace of Hong Kong. The place where the modern west meets a rapidly developing China. But in a setting where many traditional eastern customs and beliefs remain in a fusion of colour and neon and in a melting pot of culture. Sadly, for Moseley he wouldn't be seeing many of the sights. He had a job to do, one that could be very tricky for he had no idea if he was going to be able to find Lily Fung, never mind persuade her to return to London. It had been ten years since he had last been on the island. A decade was a long time and a lot of things may have changed. Therefore, he would have to refamiliarise himself with the surroundings. This is where Laurie Sullivan might be of tremendous use to him.

Before leaving London, he emailed Sullivan to tell him he was coming over. He gave him the barest details of his brief, only telling him that he was on a *misper* case. *Misper* being short for missing person. Sullivan, emailed him back within two hours to say that he would be able to meet him in a Wanchai pub called 'The Old Country' on Jaffe Road on Wednesday afternoon at two o'clock.

Following an overnight flight of twelve hours, Moseley arrived on the other side of the globe at nine clock – Hong Kong time, the following morning. He cleared customs and immigration within the hour. Rather than take the train or bus onto Hong Kong island he took a red taxi from Chek Lap Kok airport and made it into the central district of Wanchai. He was checking into the Wanchai Mandarin Garden hotel all within one and a half hours of getting through immigration.

After a couple of hours of much needed rest, Moseley was out of the hotel for one-forty in the afternoon to meet Laurie Sullivan. Despite the jet lag in his body he was determined not to waste a minute of time. He wasn't here for a sight-seeing trip; therefore, he was looking to get out and start his investigation as soon as possible. From what he could recall from his last visit, much had changed in the past decade. There were now several new high-rise buildings and more glitz, but the old commercialism was just as rampant. What hadn't changed at all was the fast pace of life and the sights, sounds and the smells of Hong Kong, the beating heart of the new assertive China on the south-east tip of the Chinese mainland.

'The Old Country' pub on Jaffe Road was a fifteen-minute stroll from his hotel, through the back-street markets of Wanchai. It was precisely two o'clock when he spotted a neon-lit sign advertising the pub, attached to the building above an entrance. He stepped off the pavement, through an opening, up a flight of steep stone stairs, through a second open door and into the bar area.

Despite being a Wednesday afternoon, the bar was full of young, business types in sharp suits, shiny shoes, and executive haircuts. Asian, European and North American voices filled the air. The talk was of business and money. Two pretty girls behind the bar were serving food and drinks to the patrons. A wide screen TV above the mirrored bar was displaying Hong Kong stock market movements. Whirling fans in the ceiling wafted a pleasant, cooling breeze throughout the interior.

Moseley put his eyes on Laurie Sullivan the instant he stepped inside. It wasn't hard to see him. Sullivan was a man of good stature who, even at sixty-five-years-of-age, hadn't lost any of his size. He was standing adjacent to the bar with a bottle in one hand and a full glass in the other.

Sullivan was originally from the Salford area where he was a detective sergeant in the Manchester force for several years before transferring to the Hong Kong police service in the mid-1980s. He had a northerner's gruff approach to life and a no-nonsense approach to what was right and what was wrong. This may have been tainted by some misdemeanours from his past. Which is why, when the opportunity arose, he had gotten out of the North of England and transferred over here. Once here he had ascended the greasy pole rapidly to become a top detective in the island's police department. He was a copper's copper in the days when a good whack across the back of the head was all a 'scallywag' required to keep him on the straight and narrow.

Moseley knew Sullivan had a reputation for being a detective who seldom played it by the book, but he was well-respected. When the British left Hong Kong in 1997, Sullivan decided to remain in post. The new police authorities thought it prudent to retain his services. He was still here twenty years later. He was, by now, fluent in Cantonese and Mandarin. At the time he was married to a local girl twenty years his junior. The marriage didn't last long. They divorced within three years. He lived in an up-market part of Kowloon, in a high-rise apartment block, Just like most of the locals.

It felt good for Moseley to see him in the flesh after three years. From what he could tell Sullivan hadn't changed all that much. He had a shaven head three years before and still had one today so that hadn't changed. As a result, he wasn't grey. He was wearing a plain, white cotton shirt, open to the second button so he was displaying a line of chest hair and a pendant on a gold chain around his neck. His skin looked waxy and his face sported the tell-tale signs of ageing. Still he wasn't a bad-looking guy even at this age.

Sullivan observed Moseley enter the bar. He had a wide smile on his face. As they met, he held out a meaty hand and they exchanged a firm handshake. "How are you?" he asked Moseley. He hadn't lost any of his strength.

"Good," he replied, "and you?"

“Can’t complain. If I did no one would take a blind bit of notice anyway.”

Sullivan laughed out loud, raised the bottle to his lips and took a swig. In the time it took to lift the bottle to his lips Moseley detected that his personality hadn’t changed. He still retained a warm personality, a dry sense of humour, wit, and inkling of self-deprecation.

“So, what brings you to Honkers?” Sullivan asked.

“Long story.”

“Okay.” Sullivan smiled. “Care to fill me in?” he asked.

“Yeah. Can do. But first let me buy you a drink. What ’you having?”

Sullivan asked for a bottle of imported Danish lager. Moseley asked the bar girl for two.

Once they had a drink in his hands Sullivan shepherded Moseley across the room to a vacant table. They stepped into an area adjacent to an open window overlooking Jaffe Road. Across the way, clothes hanging on washing lines pulled across the balconies of a run-down tenement, were motionless in a non-existent breeze. The ceiling fans were spinning to send a delightful wave of cool air around the interior. They sat in a pair of wicker chairs at a pine topped table. Sullivan looked out of the window for a moment, then back on Moseley.

“So, you’ve come all the way out here on business. What’s the score?” he asked.

“I’m here to find a girl.”

"Aren't we all?" said Sullivan, then chuckled to himself before taking a swig of his fresh beer. "Who is she?" he asked.

"Someone you might have heard of," Moseley replied.

Sullivan looked interested. "Oh right. Like who?"

"The daughter-in-law of Ho Fung. Her name is Lily Fung."

"Ho Fung. The big business bloke. I know him," Sullivan said. "I did some work for him a few years ago. And he's called you to find her?" he asked, seemingly surprised by this revelation.

Moseley didn't ask him what kind of work he had done for Ho Fung. Perhaps he would enquire later. He looked down onto the activity on the road. At the steam rising from the street side food vendors who were cooking rice and noodles to sell to the passing trade. The noise of the traffic and the sights and sounds of people on the pavement filtered their way through the open window. Moseley noticed that Sullivan's brow was peppered with beads of sweat, though it wasn't a hot day in mid-town Hong Kong.

"That's right," said Moseley responding to his question.

"What do you know about her?" Sullivan asked.

"Not a lot. I've got a photograph of her and her husband. He doesn't seem bothered about her. I picked up that vibe from the old man."

"Who doesn't seem bothered by what?"

"Her husband. Hue Fung doesn't appear to be bothered that she's gone."

"Let me see the photograph," Sullivan requested.

Moseley extracted the photograph from a jacket pocket and handed it to him. Sullivan glanced at it fleetingly. "Pretty woman. How old?" he asked.

"According to the old man she's twenty-eight."

"Twenty-eight hey?"

Moseley said nothing. He rubbed his tired eyes. He'd had several hours sleep, but the jet lag was still deeply imbedded in his head. He was suffering from a bout of Hong Kong haze and culture shock. It would take at least another twenty-four hours for it to work out of his system. He took a sip of the beer in the glass, then looked down onto the top of a double-decker tram trundling along Jaffe Road.

Sullivan handed the photograph back to him. "What did Fung tell you about her?" he asked.

"Not a great deal. Just that she's got into bed with this playboy type and returned here with him."

"Maybe the marriage was already on the rocks and she didn't need much persuasion to run off with this guy. What's his name?" Sullivan asked.

"According to Fung. He's called Leo Sinnott." Sullivan's eyebrows lifted on mention of the name. Moseley saw his reaction. "You know him?" he asked.

"I don't know him. But sure, I've heard his name and heard about his reputation."

"What reputation?" Moseley asked.

"Bit of a charismatic guy with matinee idol good looks. Rich. Well educated. Connected. Old money type. British father. Hong Kong Chinese mother. Born here in HK."

"He's a racehorse trainer," said Moseley.

"Yeah, that's him. Have you got an address for him?" Sullivan asked.

Moseley nipped his fingers into a pocket and extracted his notepad. He had written the address on the first page. He opened the notepad and looked at it. He read it out in a low voice. "Apartment 35A, Tower C, Leighton Hill, Hong Kong."

"Sounds about right. A location overlooking Happy Valley racecourse," said Sullivan. He took an intake of the beer in the bottle in his hand. "Where did he meet Lily Fung?" he asked.

"Not sure where exactly. Fung never said. All he said was that Sinnott was in England on horse racing business and met her somewhere. Swept her off her feet and persuaded her to come back here with him. Next thing she's in Hong Kong. But the old man wants her to return P.D.Q."

"P.D. what?" Sullivan asked.

"Pretty damn quick."

Sullivan chuckled. "He's got serious form of doing this kind of thing."

"Who?" Moseley asked. "What kind of thing?" he added.

"Leo Sinnott," replied Sullivan. Moseley immediately thought that Sullivan may have known Sinnott better than he was letting on. There was something in his tone and reaction that suggested he knew him well. He parked it at the back of his mind for the time-being. He looked at his notepad.

"This is the only address I've got for him. The one in Leighton Hill."

Sullivan edged forward. "I suggest you go there to see if she's there. If not, he might know where she is," he said. He took another sip of his beer and savoured the taste of the hops as they hit the back of his tongue. Then he wiped the back of his hand over his brow to dislodge the beads of sweat. His skin was glistening with perspiration and the oil on his bald head was reflecting the light.

"I think that sounds like a good suggestion. I'll start by contacting this guy to see if she's there or if he knows where she is. Thing is I might need backup. Would you watch my back?" Moseley asked.

Sullivan considered the question for a few brief moments. "Yeah. Of course. Glad to assist in any way I can. Let's go. Do it now. Strike while the iron's hot. We'll take a taxi. If he's not there he'll be at the track this evening. Wednesday night is race night at the Valley."

"Okay," said Moseley. It appeared as if Sullivan was more than happy to get involved right from the start. Moseley could only think this was a positive development.

It was a further five minutes before they stepped out of the pub and went down the stairs to street level. The sound of the street-life and the traffic on Jaffe Road bounced off the walls in the tightly packed valley of tall buildings.

On the street, water was running in the gutter to sweep litter away. The surroundings were so different to those in London. Moseley was still finding it difficult to grasp that he was in Hong Kong. It might take a few more hours for the location to really sink in.

Sullivan led the way to a taxi rank on the corner of the street. He spoke fluent Cantonese to the cab driver and asked him to take them to an address in Leighton Hill.

Chapter 4

The taxi driver soon took them out of Wanchai and the two or three miles across town to Leighton Hill. The surrounding hilltops contained a semi-circular wall of eight apartment blocks that reach up forty floors to ring the valley and encase it in a spectacular backdrop.

The high towers were in an area overlooking the large oval-shaped segment of open land that was the magnificent Happy Valley racecourse.

The cabbie set them down outside the front of apartment tower C and by a garden area in front of the glass foyer area that led into the tower. As it was on high ground, Leighton Hill afforded a spectacular view out over the skyscrapers spread across the cityscape, the harbour and the top of Victoria peak.

They got out of the cab. Sullivan paid the fare on the path. He asked the driver to hang about for ten minutes just in case they needed him to take them back. Then they stepped through a well-tended manicured garden and on towards the glass entrance. Moseley looked up the sheer face of the building soaring up forty floors with a majestic curve of its structure. In the wide balconies, turquoise-coloured blinds cascaded up like rows of perfectly-formed building blocks. Sunlight was reflecting in the windows and steel to splinter off in rays of sharp light.

Sullivan led the way through the glass sliding doors and into a foyer that had a polished marble floor. Cool air was wafting out of an air-conditioning duct. The interior was furnished with several items of artwork and fine decoration, such as several highly-decorative china vases and bottle green glass jardinières full of green leaf plants.

Across the floor was an opaque glass desk at which a man dressed in a pale blue security guard's uniform was sitting reading a newspaper. The sight of two westerners approaching the desk didn't appear to unsettle him as he continued to look at the newspaper until the men were virtually on top of him.

Sullivan gained his attention and said something in Cantonese which immediately attracted his interest. As he didn't understand one word of what was being said Moseley could only watch and listen. He was aware of a jasmine fragrance in the cool air. Sullivan and the security guard continued their conversation and even exchanged a smile and a chuckle. The words pinged around the interior and bounced off the high ceiling. On the back wall were two sets of silver-metal doors that led into elevators. The illuminated number count above the doors - from forty to zero - was lit as two cars ventured up and down the huge building. One was stationary on the 10th floor, the other was moving from the 8th floor to the ground.

Sullivan said a few words then the security guard took a telephone, prodded a four-digit number in the pad and waited for a reply.

Sullivan looked to Moseley. "He's calling Sinnott's apartment to see if he's home."

"Okay."

"He's only just come on duty," Sullivan said. He looked at his watch. "In the past fifteen minutes. He's no idea if he's at home or if he recently left."

"Did you ask him if he's recently been seen with a pretty woman?"

Sullivan smiled a toothy grin. "He's a playboy for crying out loud. He's had more women up there, than you've had hot dinners."

Twenty seconds passed. One set of the lift doors opened on the ground floor. An elderly Asian lady and a younger woman stepped out and made their way across the floor and out of the sliding-glass doors.

Before they had gone from view the security guard put the telephone down into the cradle. He looked at Sullivan and said something in Cantonese. Sullivan replied in kind and they exchanged a few more words in a pleasant manner.

"He's not here," said Sullivan, referring to Sinnott. "He said, he'll probably be at the stables at the racetrack. Tonight, is race night. He'll be at the track getting his horses prepared for the meeting."

"Okay," said Moseley. He extracted the photograph from a coat pocket. "Ask him if he's seen him with her." He also took out a roll of fifty-dollar Hong Kong notes and let the man see the wad. He peeled off three notes which were about the value of fourteen pounds Sterling "These should jog his memory." Sullivan smiled. He liked Moseley's style.

He spoke to the chap. Moseley handed him the photograph and wafted the three notes inches from his nose. The guy ran the tip of his tongue over his lips. He looked at Sullivan and spoke at a swift pace.

Sullivan translated: "Yeah, he's seen her, but not for two weeks at least. He said Sinnott brought her here, often, but he hasn't seen her for a while."

"Okay, thank him will you." Moseley said. He dropped the notes onto the open pages of the newspaper. The guard instantly whipped them up and placed them in a pants pocket.

With that done, Sullivan and Moseley walked out of the foyer, under the shade of the canopy and on towards the waiting taxi. "Let's see if he's at the track," said Moseley.

Once they were back in the red cab Sullivan asked the driver to take them to the stables at the racetrack. If Sinnott was going to be anywhere, it would be there.

The racetrack was just down the hill in the valley at the foot of the steep decline, less than five hundred yards from the complex of towers at Leighton Hill.

As the taxi was about to bypass the entrance to the stables Sullivan asked the driver to pull over and drop them outside the gates. The driver set them down by a pair of open, high wrought-iron gates that led into the stable complex. They got out of the cab. Sullivan paid the driver at the window.

A pair of seriously looking beefy guys were standing close to the entrance, preventing anyone without the requisite accreditation from getting into the courtyard. Inside the yard there was a path on the left-hand side snaking through a set of stables. The path must have led onto the racecourse proper. Several vehicles were parked in the courtyard along with a couple of horse boxes and vehicles which were plastered with the racecourse logo.

Sullivan and Moseley approached the two men. "You no come in," said one of them in broken English.

Sullivan responded in Cantonese which immediately put the chaps at ease. In the yard a young man was leading a glistening chestnut thoroughbred racehorse out of a horse box. There was a sound of activity and the sight of someone hosing down a black stallion.

The other security man joined his companion at the other side of the gate and eyed the strangers. Sullivan looked to Moseley. "Give them a hundred dollars each," he advised, "then they'll let us in. They think we're bookmakers' spies here to keep tabs on the horses. I've told them that we're just looking for Leo Sinnott. He's here okay. That's his silver Nissan parked over there," he pointed to it. Sure enough, there was a new-model Nissan Juke parked on one side of the courtyard in a line of vehicles. Moseley slipped his hand into his pocket and withdrew the roll of notes. He peeled off four fifty-dollar notes and gave them two each. They stepped aside and allowed the Englishmen to enter. The way to the racetrack was along the path in between the patchwork of stables.

They stepped across the yard, then down a path. Moseley could smell the fragrance of the turf in his nostrils, intermingled with the stench of fresh horse manure.

Sullivan led the way along the snaking path and in front of the stables in which horses were being attended to. He seemed to know where he was going or maybe he had a good sense of direction. He led Moseley down the path, by the side of the last set of stables, and they came out into a lawn area by the rails at the bottom end of the track. Over to the left, in the near distance, the huge arc of the grandstands, by the finishing line, loomed high above the track. It was a very impressive sight. The massive towers of the apartment blocks on the hills that ringed the track provided it with a spectacular backdrop that couldn't be matched by any other racecourse in the world.

Several racehorses were on the track, pounding the turf, galloping around the bend at breakneck speed. The jockeys were standing high in the stirrups, with their hands tightly clasped around the reins, as they drove the mounts over the lush turf. The hoofs, thudding into the turf, provided an authentic soundtrack. About one hundred yards away, two men were standing by the rail watching the horses fly by. One of them had a stopwatch in his hand, timing the horses as they covered a measured distance. Both men were dressed in light-coloured jodhpurs, green racing capes and both wore calf length leather jockey boots.

One of them turned his head to observe Sullivan and Moseley coming their way. The horses were now just turning onto the straight leading to the finishing line. The two men parted company and one of them began to walk along the rail at a slow pace. His eyes were still on the stopwatch in his hand. The other one remained resting his arms on the top of the rail.

"Is that Leo Sinnott?" asked Moseley to Sullivan.

"Don't know," he said. But maybe he did. There was something almost manufactured about this or maybe he had just got lucky. They strode across to the guy who looked to his right as another pair of thoroughbreds came hurtling by. Moseley took the shades from his eyes. He had to blink several times then pause to let his eyes adjust to the bright colours and the power of the sunlight. Sullivan raised his voice and said something in Cantonese.

The man at the rail turned his head and looked at them.

"Hello," he said in English. He was a tall man. At least six feet in stature, slim, long-legged and barrel-chested. His jet-black hair was neatly arranged. Thick on top, less so down the sides. The fringe was pushed up in a modern style. He had a polished, sophisticated look. With mixed Caucasian and Oriental colouring and features, he resembled a handsome, glossy-magazine male model. He had the gold band of a Rolex on his right-hand wrist and a thin gold choker around his neck. He was wearing tortoise-shell frame shades over his eyes. He looked well turned out in a red-pink Polo shirt under the green cape that was closed at the neck.

"Are you Leo Sinnott?" Moseley asked, pronouncing his surname: sin not. The man didn't respond immediately. "Mr Sinnott?" Moseley asked again.

The expression on his face told Moseley he had located Leo Sinnott. Sinnott's eyes went from Moseley to Sullivan then back again. He looked slightly fearful as if he felt that something nasty was about to happen to him.

"Who are you gentlemen?" he asked.

"My name is David Moseley. This is Laurie Sullivan." Sinnott's stony, inquisitive glare didn't change. "I've come from London on the request of my client Mister Ho Fung to find his daughter-in-law, Lily Fung," said Moseley.

A mention of the name seemed to have an instant effect on Sinnott. He took a hesitant step back and the tense, stony look in his eyes intensified. His body language, which was already taut, became even more palsied.

"Do you know where she is?" Moseley asked him.

"I haven't seen her for several weeks," Sinnott said.

"So, you do know her?" Moseley asked.

"Yes. I know her. But I've not seen her for days."

"How long precisely?"

Sinnott looked at Moseley, raised himself and cocked his head back as if to make himself taller and to seek an advantage over him, though he was already two inches taller than Moseley. "Who are you?" he asked.

"Dave Moseley. I'm a private investigator sent here by Mr Fung to find his daughter-in-law."

"I know her, but she left," Sinnott said.

"Where did she go?" Moseley asked.

"I don't know," Sinnott clamped his lips together as if he wasn't going to say another word unless someone was going to make him talk.

"You don't know where she is?" Moseley asked.

"She left my place. I haven't seen her since," Sinnott said after the briefest of pauses.

"Well, she's not back in London. So, she must still be here in Hong Kong," Moseley said.

"As I say. She left my apartment with her possessions. I have no idea where she went."

"Why would she leave?" Moseley asked.

Sinnott shrugged his shoulders. "We didn't hit it off," he replied in a blasé tone.

"Did you know she's Ho Fung's daughter-in-law?" Moseley asked.

"Yes."

"So, you've no idea where she is?" Moseley asked.

"No."

"Could she be with friends?"

"Might be." Sinnott said in a cold tone. He had quickly recovered his composure and seemed happy to engage in conversation.

"Do you know any of her friends?" Moseley asked.

"No."

Moseley immediately sensed that this case was going to get a whole lot more complex than he wanted it to. Simply finding her and asking her to accompany him back to London, seemed a lot more unlikely than it did two hours before. “Did you have a falling out?” he asked.

“A what?” Sinnott asked.

“An argument. A fight of some description.”

“No.”

“You sure?”

“Of course.”

“So why did she go?” Moseley asked.

“That’s what you’ll need to ask her. She went on her own free will,” said Sinnott.

“When?”

“On the night of the twenty-ninth of March.”

“How do you know it was that night? How can you be so precise?” Moseley asked.

“It was a race night,” Sinnott replied.

“Today is the twelfth. So, she’s being gone fourteen days.”

“When I returned home that evening she had gone and taken her things with her,” Sinnott said.

This seemed to tie in with what the security guard in the building had said. He said he hadn’t seen her for two weeks.

“Okay,” said Moseley. “She’s gone but do you know where?”

“No,” Sinnott said unequivocally.

“How do I know she’s not tied up in your apartment.”

Sinnott gave him a bemused face and sought to chuckle, but pulled back from doing so. On first impressions, it looked as if he was on the level. "Why would I do that?" he asked.

"I don't know. Maybe it's something you do to pretty women." Moseley said. Sinnott grinned. "What if we check your apartment to see if she's still there," Moseley asked.

He had effectively backed Sinnott into a corner with no way out, other than to agree to take them to his home to let them look inside his apartment. Maybe Moseley would find some evidence of her existence and where she might have gone. It was an outside chance, but one he wanted to take. Sinnott considered it for a few moments. "All right. First, I'll change," he said.

"Be my guest," said Moseley.

Sinnott stepped around them. Sullivan and Moseley followed him across the lawn and over to the stable block. Moseley didn't know how this was going to pan out. There seemed to be a whole lot more to this missing person case then he had anticipated.

As they came into the yard there was a lot more activity than there had been ten minutes before. The number of horse boxes had increased two-fold and there were now more stable lads and lasses leading horses around the yard. Several stable girls in their colourful equestrian gear were carrying buckets of water towards the stables. Several men in jockey silks were standing close-by chatting. As this was a Wednesday it was race night at Happy Valley, clearly the activity in preparation of the first race at seven-thirty was in full swing.

Sinnott entered a block at the end of a row of stables and went out of sight. There was a sign which said: 更衣室 , then the English translation saying: Changing Room.

Moseley and Sullivan waited on the outside for him to emerge. Nothing was said. Moseley had an awful, deflated feeling that this enquiry could quickly spiral out of control. For the first time, he seriously considered that it was likely he would be returning to London without Lily Fung

Chapter 5

After a wait of about ten minutes, Leo Sinnott emerged from the changing room. He had changed into a pair of chinos and had a pink cashmere jumper draped over his shoulders. He still had the tortoise-shell sunglasses over his eyes. He was carrying an expensive looking brown leather sports grip in his hand.

He looked at Moseley and Sullivan. "We'll go in my car," he said. He led them to a top-of-the-range silver-grey Nissan 4x4, opened the driver's door and got in. Sullivan and Moseley got into the back and immediately breathed in the fragrance of brand-new leather.

He started the engine, backed the vehicle into the yard, did a three-point turn and headed through the open gates and out onto the busy Wanchai Road. Nothing was said.

It didn't take Sinnott long to drive up the steep incline to the Leighton Hill tower complex and head along the same service road the taxi had taken. This time he took a turn off, drove around to the back of the towers then along another service road. After fifty yards or so he drove to the back of the huge tower looming high above, to a gated entrance that led into a ground-floor car park, under tower C.

Once there he pulled up, put the window down, reached out and punched a five-digit number into an electronic number-pad. The metal gate at the entrance began to wind up. When it was all the way up, he drove through the opening and into the car park. He drove to the far side, put the vehicle into an allocated parking spot and killed the engine.

He opened his door, Sullivan and Moseley did likewise and they followed him across the smooth concrete floor to an elevator. It wasn't long before the lift arrived at the bottom floor. Sinnott directed it to the thirty-fifth floor of the forty-storey tower.

Once the lift was on the thirty-fifth floor, Sinnott turned right and led them onto a landing that was covered by a red and burgundy patterned carpet that ran from one side of the building to the other. Moseley was aware of the same cool air and the scent of jasmine. The same smell in the foyer, thirty-five floors below. Sinnott's apartment was the last door on the left-hand side of the corridor.

He punched a number into a number-pad, opened the door and led them into his apartment. It opened straight into an open plan lounge. The first thing that struck Moseley was the incredible view of the city from a high window that ran along the length of the lounge.

The interior was gorgeous. The furniture and fittings were of the highest quality. From the blanch-white leather, circular sofa in the centre of the lounge to the modern Kandinsky style artwork on the walls. Everything oozed wealth, class and good taste. All the light fittings were silver stainless steel. The apartment's key selling point was the view of the high-rise blocks and office buildings in the central district of the island. In the gaps between the skyscrapers it was possible to see a stretch of water in Victoria harbour and beyond that the spread of Kowloon towards the Chinese mainland disappearing into the distance.

Moseley took in the view. Behind the window was a balcony, an iron rail balustrade then a drop of thirty-four floors to the top of the entrance canopy roof on the ground level.

Sinnott put his sports bag on a side table aside of the sofa. He went to a telephone and pressed a button. It told him he had three new messages. He elected not to listen to any of them.

Moseley looked around. Nothing was out of place. A huge widescreen TV was attached to the far wall. A set of six tall bulrushes were in a large earthenware glazed clay pot. There was no evidence of a fight or anything remotely like that. Several doors led into rooms off the main living area.

"What do you want to see?" Sinnott asked.

"Everything," Moseley replied.

"I've nothing to hide. She's not here." Moseley could see there was no evidence that she was here. "You can tell Mr Fung. She's not here," Sinnott said in a calm tone.

"Okay. I'll do that once I'm satisfied," said Moseley. "What's that room?" he asked thrusting his chin to a closed door.

Sinnott didn't reply. He went to the door and opened it. Moseley followed him into a master bedroom that was furnished in a kind of seventies explosion of colour. Reds and crimsons, shades of apricot and pinks were dominant. The bed was king size. It was neatly made up. Half a dozen pillows were arranged across the bottom of a semi-circular head-board. There was a thick, fluffy carpet on the floor. A door led into an en-suite powder room.

Moseley glanced around the room. She wasn't in there. Next Sinnott took him into the main apartment bathroom. It was decked out in black ceramic tiles, glass and chrome. There was a fancy heart-shaped bath with water jets inserted into the surface. A set of snow-white towels were arranged on a ten-bar high stainless-steel heated rail. Glass shelves were lined with several male-grooming products. Moseley noticed the lack of female products.

From the bathroom, Sinnott took him into a kitchen. It looked as if he didn't eat-in often because everything was spotlessly clean and looked virtually unused. It was a bachelor pad all right. Of course, Moseley knew it didn't mean to say he wouldn't have another place elsewhere. Still this was the address he had been given. There was absolutely no evidence of a female presence here.

Sinnott showed him the rest of the apartment. She wasn't here, nor was there any evidence to say she had. The security guard had said she was here for two weeks. Therefore, she had gone elsewhere.

Sinnott ushered Moseley back into the lounge area where Sullivan was standing by the window, enjoying the magnificent view of the city. Down below the horseshoe shape racetrack, the stands and the stables were picture-postcard magnificent. On the balcony, the petals of a child's windmill were turning at a furious pace as the humid air, hit a high, at three o'clock in the afternoon.

"You can see she's not here," said Sinnott. "I don't know where she is." He sounded genuine. "She'd been here, but then she went." It would appear that the handsome, rich playboy, race-horse trainer was telling the truth.

"I believe you," said Moseley, "and thanks for showing me around," he added.

Laurie Sullivan turned away from the window and came into the centre of the room.

"Let's go," he said looking at Moseley.

Sullivan led the way to the main door of the apartment. Sinnott didn't move from the spot. Sullivan stepped out onto the landing and headed towards the elevator doors. Moseley was a few paces behind him.

The fact that Sullivan seemed to know where he was going wasn't lost on Moseley. It could have been down to his 'copper's nose' or maybe he had been in a similar building to this or in this very block in the past. After all, he was a detective in the Hong Kong police for longer than Moseley had been a detective in the Met. He didn't think a great deal about it.

They were at the lift in a few moments. They rode down to the ground floor and out into the warmth of the mid-afternoon sunlight blazing into the foyer.

Sullivan spoke a few words to the guy at the reception desk. He picked up a telephone and tapped in a number. A taxi to take them into central Wanchai arrived five minutes later.

Chapter 6

The taxi driver dropped Moseley right outside his hotel in Wanchai. Sullivan said he was going on to the Star ferry terminal for a leisurely boat ride across the harbour to Kowloon.

Moseley entered the hotel and took the lift to his room on the twentieth floor. Unfortunately, the view from the room wasn't as stunning as the one Leo Sinnott enjoyed. The view from this one looked straight out onto the face of a dilapidated residential tower block. Once in his room he sat in a chair at a writing desk, relaxed and spent the following few minutes pondering his next move.

The last couple of hours had been somewhat of a whirlwind experience. Something wasn't right. Something was very wrong, but he couldn't put his finger on it. Here he was half way around the world, looking for someone who may not exist. Something in the back of his mind told him that it was too smooth, that it was all stage-managed. Moseley had his doubts about Sullivan too, but didn't have a clear inkling why he was thinking like that. Maybe it was just his thought process in flux, putting two and two together and coming up with five.

What he did suspect was that Sinnott's apartment was too clean and sanitised. Almost too perfect to be true. No one could live in such a dust free space, but maybe he did. Maybe he didn't. Had someone been brought in to clean the apartment from top to bottom to remove all traces of Lily Fung? Had Sinnott been too accommodating and too insistent that she wasn't there. The sense of stage management was strong. Moseley knew that he had to get Sinnott alone and interrogate him one-on-one. Perhaps his chance would come later that evening at the Happy Valley racetrack, for Wednesday night was race night. As he was a horse trainer, Sinnott would be meeting jockeys and others in the parade ring. This could be his one and only chance to meet him face-to-face in order to put some questions to him.

For now, he took a shower, slipped on a warm fluffy bathrobe, laid on the bed and took a nap. The residues of the long flight were still in his system and he was fighting the fatigue that had clamped tightly around his body, nulled his brain and put all kinds of weird stumbling thoughts into his head. His mind was still in kind of a daze, brought on by suffocating jet-lag.

At just after six-thirty on a pleasant Hong Kong evening Moseley left the hotel. He took a taxi from a rank outside the hotel and asked the driver to take him to the Happy Valley racetrack.

Race night at Happy Valley was something to behold. The course was renowned for its atmosphere, fine dining, and the buzz of excitement as a dozen thoroughbred race horses came galloping down the final straight, under the glare of floodlights, with the roar of the crowd in the background.

Moseley got to the track at seven o'clock and joined a queue at the ten dollars 'tourist' pay gate. Once inside he made his way into the spectator area and joined the crowd, most of whom were locals.

If there is one thing that a lot of Hong Kong Chinese enjoy doing, then it's a flutter on a horse race at Happy Valley. In one night, literally millions of Hong Kong dollars are gambled on the outcomes of the eight-race card.

On a Wednesday night in April the arena was buzzing. The grandstands were already packed when the horses appeared on the track and came into the parade ring for the first race at seven-thirty. As darkness was falling the floodlights illuminating the track were at full strength to splash light over the verdant green of the turf. In the high-rise tower's lights were beaming out of the glass and metal blocks like pin-pricks of colour suspended in the dark sky.

Moseley paid the two dollars for a race-card then joined the rest of the punters on a stretch of ground near to the finishing post. The majority of those on the terrace below the huge grandstands were consulting racing papers.

A huge TV on the other side of the track was showing the action from previous race meetings. The sound of commentaries was playing over the public address. Neon figures displaying the forecast betting patterns, on a huge board across on the other side of the track, were changing in the blink of an eye. In the betting halls, the spectators were putting their hard-earned cash onto their fancied mounts.

The first race was due off shortly. By the time Moseley got to the parade ring the horses were being led round the circle by stable lads and lasses. Several of the jockeys, in their colourful racing silks, were already in the centre of the ring talking to trainers, owners, and the connections.

Moseley consulted the race card. He wasn't into horse racing so he didn't understand the terminology and the language. But he wasn't here to gamble on the races, therefore it wasn't a problem. He was here to find and speak to Leo Sinnott.

He slipped the race card into a jacket pocket, made his way through the crowd gathered close to the finishing line, and walked around the outside of the parade ring. The evening had turned warm, and the floodlights were giving off a residual heat. The fragrance of spicy food cooking in a mobile kitchen made his mouth water. The race announcer came over the public address and welcomed the spectators to the meeting. The atmosphere was building. Punters were coming out of the hospitality suites in the grandstands to watch the horses being led out of the ring and onto a cinder track to parade in front of the stands.

Moseley stopped at the top of the parade ring and leaned against the rail. He looked at the race card, at the list of runners and riders for the first race. Like any other race card, the world over, it listed the name of the horse, its form over the past five races, the jockey, the trainer, and the owner's name, whether it be an individual owner, a family or a syndicate.

The first race was a six-furlong dash for two-year-old maidens. He carried on around the ring to a point where he could see the horses parading on the cinder track in front of the punters, then they turned onto the turf, picked up speed and trotted down to the starting stalls at the bottom of the long straight.

In the stand the number of spectators standing on the concrete steps of the terracing had increased so there were few free spaces.

When all the horses were in the stalls, a bell sounded and the announcer declared, *they're off.* The big screen showed the action as the horses put on the turbo and came thundering up the finishing straight. The crowd roared as they approached the final furlong. The intensity of the sound of the hoofs thudding against the turf increased in velocity as the nags neared the finishing post. The sight of eight thoroughbred race horses galloping at full pace under the floodlights was magnificent. There wasn't another racetrack in the world to match the majestic Happy Valley.

The first of the eight races was over in no time at all. The winner, number three: 'Sacred Heart', prevailed by a short head.

The second race was due to get under way at eight o'clock. Moseley looked at his watch; the time was twenty to the hour. The horses for the second race would be parading in the ring in ten minutes. He had some time to kill before the next race, so he did what most of the locals and tourists were doing and that was to visit one of the bars inside one of the track-side beer tents, for like the British, the Hong Kong Chinese loved a beer every now and again.

In contrast to the frenzy on the track-side the atmosphere inside the beer tent was tranquil. The dominant language was Cantonese although a few English accents could be heard.

Moseley purchased a pint of amber nectar and jostled for a position at a table to put his beer down. He looked at the runners and riders for the second race, a one-mile sprint for three-year-old geldings. He ran his eyes down the list of horses. What caught his attention was horse number eight. A horse by the name of 'Steel Rapier'. Rider: Mike Fallon, Trainer: Leo Sinnott. What he read next made him gulp. The owner was 'Ho Fung Belgravia Racing Consortium.' *Oh, my word,* he said to himself. Here was a sign from above. It was like a thunderbolt hitting home. A tangible connection between the owner and the trainer. Though they were six thousand miles apart here was a connection that linked two of the key players in this affair; the trainer and the owner had a connection to each other.

It was standard practice for the owner of a horse or his or her representative to meet with the trainer before the race in the parade ring for the trainer to brief the connections. In this case Ho Fung wouldn't be here. Still Moseley knew that he had a chance to meet with Sinnott, face-to-face and ask him some questions.

At a quarter to eight a bell sounded which told the punters that the horses were about to enter the ring. Moseley stepped out of the beer tent and into the area in front of the ring. The horses were being led along the cinder track. This was one of the feature races of the evening, a group one race for thoroughbreds, with the first past the post picking up a purse of four hundred and seventy-five thousand Hong Kong dollars. A straight mile from the stalls at the bottom of the track to the finishing post in front of the stands.

Moseley made it along the rail to the opening into the parade ring where two suited security guards were checking the credentials of those seeking to gain access. Some horse owners and their guests, or better known as the connections, were already in the ring talking to the jockeys and the trainers. He observed the scene for a few moments then a line of horses began to come through a gate at the cinder track and into the ring.

Moseley watched the activity. Most of the people were in groups of five or six. There were eight horses in this race. Therefore, eight sets of connections. The jockeys emerged from the weighing room and made their way into the ring. Moseley couldn't see Leo Sinnott from this spot, but then a group of people moved away and he saw Sinnott, standing, talking to a group of four people.

Sinnott was in a sharp-cut suit, shirt, and tie. He was wearing his shades. He looked every inch the sophisticated lady-killer and playboy of Hong Kong society and the darling of the Happy Valley jet-set. Moseley decided to take a chance. He dropped his head, looked at his race card and approached the gate where the connections were going through. The two men closed the gap, looked at him and searched for the purple badge attached to his jacket to indicate he had the necessary accreditation. He looked for all the world like a journalist and not an owner. Moseley eyed them then looked at his race card.

"I'm the representative of the owner of Steel Rapier. Horse number eight," he said in a convincing manner. The two guys looked at each other, but didn't want to challenge him and ask him who he was. The more assertive-looking one stepped aside and allowed Moseley to walk past him and enter the parade ring. He made straight across the lawn for Leo Sinnott who was standing in the centre watching his mount circling the ring. Moseley was upon him in a couple of strides. Sinnott turned to see Moseley coming towards him. At the same moment one of the jockeys came walking up to him. Sinnott's gaze didn't waver.

"Good evening," said Moseley as cool as you like. Sinnott was shocked to see him this close and could only mutter "Ah, just a minute. I need to talk to my jockey," he said.

"Not a problem," replied Moseley and stepped back a pace.

He could hear Sinnott and the jockey have a short conversation about the tactics for the race, then the jockey moved away from him to leave Sinnott and Moseley alone. The group of four people, Sinnott was previously talking to, were drifting off to the exit to get to their seats high in the grandstand.

"What do you want?" Sinnott asked with an edge of irk in the tone.

"You know where she is. Don't you?"

Sinnott glanced from side to side as if looking for someone to come to his aid. He must have calculated that shouting out for help or causing a scene would only draw attention to himself. He wasn't going to make a song and dance in front of the people in the ring. He turned his body full on to Moseley and fronted up. He whipped the shades off his eyes and fixed them on Moseley with a stare.

"I don't," he replied bluntly to Moseley's question.

"What don't you know?" Moseley asked.

"Where she is," Sinnott replied.

"You must know Ho Fung well. He's a racehorse owner. He owns the horse you're training in this race."

"Yes. I know him. I never said I didn't," said Sinnott with a shrug of his shoulders.

"Did you meet him in London?" Moseley asked. Sinnott rang a hand across his mouth and his eyes darted around the ring. He was ill at ease and his body language was tense. "Did you meet her in London?" Moseley asked.

"Who?"

"Lily Fung?"

"Yes."

"Why?"

"Why what?"

"Why did you target her?"

Sinnott must have sensed that Moseley was far more clued up than he had anticipated. "I was paid to," he replied.

"You were paid to bring her here?" Moseley asked.

"Yes."

"By whom?"

"Ho Fung, of course," Sinnott said, as if Moseley should have known the answer to the question.

"Why?" Moseley asked.

Sinnott shrugged his shoulders. Then his eyes went to a horse as it suddenly reared up. The stable lad leading the animal was able to get it back under control.

A bell sounded and the lads and lasses brought their horses into the centre of the ring.

"Just a minute," Sinnott said. With that he stepped away from Moseley and went to the horse, where the jockey was now standing, checking the straps holding the saddle in place. The jockey presented his leg to Sinnott, who took it and gave him a leg-up. The jockey swung into the saddle, placed his feet into the stirrups and took the reins in both hands. Meanwhile, the numbers on the neon illuminated totaliser on the other side of the track were turning over at a rapid rate. Money was pouring onto the runners. The favoured bet appeared to be a dual forecast on horses three and seven.

The first of the horses left the parade ring and went out onto the cinder track to parade in front of the grandstand. A buzz of anticipation increased in velocity.

Moseley watched Sinnott come back towards him. He looked very cool in his expensive suit and the shades. The revelation that Fung had paid him to bring his daughter-in-law back to Hong Kong, caught Moseley by surprise. He had no idea why he would do that.

Sinnott was soon next to him. "I don't understand," Moseley said.

"What?" Sinnott asked.

"Why would Fung ask me to find her if he paid you to bring her here?"

Sinnott shrugged his shoulders for a second time. “No idea,” he replied.

“Is her marriage to his son on the rocks?”

“What do you mean?”

“Is their marriage in some sort of trouble?”

“How would I know?” he replied.

“Fung paid you to get her out of London?”

“Yes.”

“Where is she now?” Moseley asked.

“Pardon me.”

“Where is she now?” he repeated forcefully.

“I don’t know,” Sinnott replied in a tiresome tone. He watched the first of the eight horses turn off the cinder track and canter down to the starting stalls at the bottom of the straight. The huge TV screen on the other side of the track monitored the horses going down to the start.

“How long was she with you?” Moseley asked.

“As I said earlier. Two weeks at the most.”

“Did she know Ho Fung had paid you to entice her away from London?”

Sinnott pursed his lips. “I don’t think so.”

“Did she leave a forwarding address anywhere?” Moseley asked.

“I would have told you if she had.”

“Why do you think Fung wanted her back here?”

“No idea,” replied Sinnott.

"Okay," said Moseley. He was even more puzzled now, though he knew he couldn't do much more than take Sinnott at his word. If Sinnott was telling the truth and he had little doubt that he wasn't, then her whereabouts was a mystery. "Does she have many friends here?" he asked.

"I don't know," Sinnott replied.

"What was her name before she married Hue Fung?"

Sinnott looked at him as if it was a trick question. "I don't know." Moseley concluded he didn't know much about anything.

The race commentator came over the PA and became embroiled in a chit-chat with a colleague who went through the form-guide of the horses for the second race. 'Steel Rapier' was mentioned a couple of times, but it was low down in the list of fancied runners. The favourite was horse number three, 'Shanghai Knight', at odds of nine-to-two, with 'Court Jester', number seven, second favourite at five-to-one.

Moseley could see that Sinnott was eager to get to the rail to watch the race, so he backed off. "Thanks for fronting up," he said

"What's that mean?" Sinnott asked.

"Nothing," said Moseley.

The commentator came over the public address to tell the crowd that the horses were about to be placed into the stalls for the second race.

"Thanks for your time," Moseley said, but Sinnott didn't hear him above the clamour of sound coming from the crowd.

Not for the first-time Moseley thought that the chances of leaving Hong Kong with Lily Fung on a plane bound for London were much less than fifty-fifty. His only hope was to ask Laurie Sullivan if he could ask some of his contacts in the HK police if they knew where she was residing.

Moseley left the racecourse before the second race started. He took a cab back to Wanchai.

Chapter 7

The streets of Wanchai were busy with activity on this Wednesday night. Since the 1997 changeover the area had lost most of its edgy character following a period of forced gentrification. There weren't half as many bars offering passers-by the opportunity to enter a hostess run establishment, as there once were. They were traps in which some naive victim would be charged large amounts of money for the cheapest of drinks.

As Moseley entered into the glass entrance of his hotel and the wide-open floor of the foyer, he glanced towards the desk were several members of staff were standing. One of the senior clerks at the concierge desk saw him and immediately raised his hand and beckoned Moseley towards the desk. He had a serious urgent look on his face.

Moseley acknowledged him with a vague nod of the head then stepped across the floor towards the desk. He had no idea what he wanted. The chap was a medium build, nice-looking, slim middle-aged man in a freshly-pressed jacket with the hotel logo and emblem on the breast pocket.

There was a nervous smile on his face. He looked as if he was about to give Moseley some bad news. No one back home knew he was here, therefore it wasn't likely to be a message to call home or anything like that.

"Mr Mos-el-ey," said the chap. "Please wait here for one moment."

Moseley didn't reply. He could only do as asked as thoughts went through his mind. He wondered if his credit card had been rejected. The chap turned away, went along the back of the desk and through an open door. He emerged several moments later with an older, more senior hotel employee leading the way. He too wore a frown.

The older chap approached him alone and came towards the desk. He held his hand out. He was a short, mildly-overweight guy, wearing silver-rimmed spectacles. His hair was grey and swept back to reveal a thinning patch on his forehead. Before Moseley could take his hand, the chap took his glasses off. Moseley took his hand. It was meaty and sweaty and his body language was stiff, but his handshake was firm and strong.

"My name is Mr Lee. I'm the hotel security manager. I'm so sorry," he said.

Moseley narrowed his eyes. "Sorry. About what?" he asked.

"Perhaps we should go into your room."

"Why? What's in my room?"

"Someone has broken in and looked through your things," the man said.

Moseley was stunned. "Broken in!" he exclaimed incredulously.

"That's what it looks like," Mr Lee said.

"Oh, my word," was Moseley's somewhat under-stated response.

"I will accompany you to your room. We will, of course, reimburse you for your trouble."

Moseley didn't say anything. He was in a quandary. This was a five-star hotel. Things like this were only supposed to happen in budget hotels. The reality was that they could occur anywhere. Here was the proof.

Mr Lee stepped along the back of the counter, through a flap at the end and came onto the foyer. Moseley followed him across the floor to the bank of lifts. There were a few people sitting in an arrangement of seats set around walnut topped circular tables near to a concessionary snack and beverage outlet. Some were chatting in conversation. Others reading newspapers or eating and drinking. A large screen TV was airing a twenty-four-hour English language news channel. It was standard in any large hotel anywhere in the world. Moseley couldn't help but wonder if one of those sitting there was responsible for what he would find in his room. Then he wondered if the burglar had got access into the safe and stolen his money, passport and other valuables. He didn't want to think of the consequences if his possessions were no longer in the room.

Mr Lee led Moseley into an elevator and they travelled up to the twentieth floor in silence.

As Moseley emerged out of the car and stepped onto the long landing, he could see a hotel employee standing outside the door to his room, guarding it. The door was open. Mr Lee took Moseley into the room. A second man, another hotel employee, was already inside the room, standing by the window with the view out to the high-rise tenement building across the way.

It was clear to see that someone had been in the room, emptied his clothes out of two bedside drawers and scattered most of them onto the mattress and over the floor. The bed clothes had been stripped off the mattress which was lying at an angle, half on - half off the bed frame. Whoever it was had clearly been looking for something under the mattress. Moseley went to the wardrobe. The door was hanging open. When he looked down to the safe unit, he could see that the door was closed. He got down on his knees, took the handle and pulled on it. Thankfully, it was still locked. He let out a sigh of relief. The burglar hadn't been able to get into the safe, therefore his money, passport and other valuables were still inside. "At least they didn't get into here," he said.

"Pardon me. They?" said Mr Lee.

"He. She. It. They." Moseley said in a barbed tone. He tried the flap again, just to make sure it was locked, then he tapped the four-digit code into the pad. The mechanism buzzed and the door popped open. He put his hand inside and felt his possessions which were still in place. Maybe the burglar was disturbed before he could get into the safe. As it was bolted into the floor, it would have been near impossible to pull it free unless he had his hands on a drill of some description to unscrew the bolts.

Moseley got to his feet. He was at a loss to explain why anyone would want to break into the room, but obviously someone had. Was it something to do with the assignment he was on? He didn't want to begin jumping to conclusions or speculate at this early stage. However, no one breaks into a hotel room without good reason, unless it was an opportunist thief. Perhaps a chancer had walked in off the street, tried his hand, and chose this room at random.

The other chap in the room was a hotel employee. He was perhaps a couple of years younger than Mr Lee. He was a small, shifty-looking guy with nicotine-stained fingers and slightly bulbous dark eyes which held a menacing quality. He picked up the discarded bed sheets then nudged the mattress back onto the frame.

Moseley looked at the security manager. "Who found the room and when?" he asked.

"My colleague here," said Lee gesturing to the chap who was now picking up some of the discarded clothing from the floor. "At just after eight o'clock this evening." Moseley looked at his watch. The time was eight-thirty. He had left the room close to two hours before. Just forty minutes before he was talking to Leo Sinnott at the track. Sinnott would have had plenty of time to call someone to tell him that Moseley was there asking him questions. Maybe the burglary was a kind of warning.

Moseley stepped to the main door and examined the lock. There was no evidence that the door had been forced open. Whoever had come in must have used a replica key-card to trigger the opening mechanism. The explanation was simple. The burglar was either looking for valuables or a specific item of interest, such as the photograph of Lily Fung and her husband.

“We are most sorry for this disturbance,” said Mr Lee in an earnest tone. “We will of course move you to another room. Has anything being taken?” he asked.

Moseley looked around. “Not that I can see,” he replied.

“He’s a chance burglar,” said Lee.

“Has anyone else being targeted tonight or in the past few days?” Moseley asked.

“Not that I am aware,” Lee replied.

“I don’t think it was a chance burglar then,” said Moseley.

“Why?” asked Lee.

Moseley realised he was saying too much. “Just a hunch,” he replied as if he was trying to lessen the implication of his suggestion.

Lee offered him a frown, then forced a meek grin. “We will provide you with a deluxe room,” he looked out of the window to the side of the high-rise tenement block. “On an upper floor,” he added.

Moseley didn’t reply. He was still trying to figure out the ramifications of coming back to the hotel to discover his room ransacked. He still had no way of knowing if it was in anyway connected to his investigation into the case of the *misper* Lily Fung, or if it was a pure coincidence. It was becoming almost too sinister for words.

Lee said something in Cantonese to the other fellow who had now picked up the items of clothing from the floor and had laid them all onto the mattress. Mr Lee looked at Moseley.

“I will take you to your new room. When you are ready of course. I will be waiting outside.”

Lee and the other chap stepped out of the room and left Moseley to pack his suitcase, empty the safe, collect all his belongings and put them into his case. He felt like he should be checking out, rather than agreeing to remain here, but at least they had offered him another room. As he wasn't due to check out until Monday. He still had four nights to stay. Four nights to find Lily Fung, though he suspected he wouldn't find her.

Over the course of the following five minutes he put all his clothing and items into his case and emptied the safe, then he left the room. Mr Lee was waiting for him on the landing. He took Moseley to the lift and escorted him to a suite on the fortieth floor.

It wasn't so much as another room but a massive change. The suite had a separate sitting room, and a spacious bedroom twice the size of the one he had just left, a deluxe bathroom and a view of the city that could only be seen in the TV programmes of the lifestyles of the rich and famous.

Once settled in the room he raided the free mini-bar and had a couple of miniature bottles of whisky. At a time, just before midnight he put in a call to Laurie Sullivan and asked him to meet him the next day. They arranged to meet in 'The Old Country' pub on Jaffe Road at one o'clock in the afternoon. He didn't mention anything about the meeting with Leo Sinnott or the break-in to his room. He was certain he wouldn't be visited for a second time, still it was with a sense of heightened security that he settled down for the night. Out there, across the spread of the city and over the harbour, the neon and the lights of Kowloon blinked and twinkled on the water in the harbour well into the early hours of Thursday morning.

Chapter 8

Moseley woke up at eight o'clock to the sight of grey-leaden skies over Hong Kong. A stiff wind was splattering heavy raindrops against the window. Out over the harbour the backdrop of Kowloon was hidden behind a bank of mist and fog that might remain static for most of the day. The water in the harbour was so choppy white-capped waves were sent crashing against the harbour wall.

The previous night, the weather girl on the English language CNN TV channel had told the viewers that a twenty-four-hour storm would come over the entire south-east peninsula of the Chinese mainland. The storm should clear out by this time tomorrow. The coming weekend was going to be fine with the first day of higher temperatures coming in on Saturday. Still the storm was no-way as bad as some of the typhoons that the city had to endure during the monsoon season when the New Territories and the island went into virtual lockdown and very few people, other than the foolhardy, ventured out.

Moseley had no intention of staying in the hotel. He was going out at one o'clock to visit the 'The Old Country' pub to meet with Laurie Sullivan. He showered then went into the restaurant for breakfast with the other several hundred guests. The ramifications of last night were still playing heavily on his mind. He couldn't help but think that one of the hotel staff had a duplicate key-card and used it to gain access to the room, searched through his belongings looking for something, couldn't find it, then raised the alarm. Maybe it was the other chap who had been in the room when he entered with Mr Lee. He just didn't know. If it was him, who had told him to do it? As he glanced around the restaurant at the other guests eating breakfast, he couldn't help but wonder if one of them had done the deed. He felt himself becoming suspicious of everyone, which in truth didn't help him to deal with it. The fact that the safe hadn't been opened, suggested to him that it wasn't anybody who had access to the rooms. Perhaps it was an opportunist thief who had walked in off the street, evaded the security measures and managed to get up to the twentieth floor unchallenged.

During the telephone conversation with Laurie Sullivan, he had purposely refrained from mentioning the break-in. Something in the back of his mind pointed to a connection. As a detective, his mind was trained to look for connections. Maybe there was a modicum of connectivity here, though he conceded it could be his inbuilt analytical thinking that encouraged an inquisitive retrospective review of all the variables. He knew that the majority of crimes had an element of causation link. All criminologists know that most crimes have linkage and are committed by a person known to the victim.

His breakfast consisted of little more than a small bowl of cereal, coffee, fruit and juice. He planned to have something more substantial at lunch time when he met with Sullivan in the pub on Jaffe Road.

By midday the skies were beginning to clear and the strength of the wind had dropped. The storm was downgraded from a force seven – moderate gale – to a force five – a fresh breeze.

Moseley left the hotel at a few minutes to one. He decided to approach the pub from a different direction. He made his way onto Hennessey Road and to the long line of stores that are famed for selling gold and jewellery. He crossed the road at a busy crossing and came onto Jaffe Road, then along the pavement for fifty yards, then up the concrete steps to the first floor, through the open door and into the pub with its pine tables, wicker chairs and low-slung, leather sofas. The ceiling fans were spinning at a gentle rotation. The long glass mirror behind the counter and the lines of liquor bottles gleamed in the light.

The open windows, were partially covered by slattered wooden shutters so it was only just possible to hear the activity on the street below. The room was frequented by a dozen or so people. A few tourists, along with office workers from the nearby businesses. The smell and sight of chilli bubbling in a large cooking pot and chicken breasts rotating on skewers in an oven made Moseley's mouth water.

Laurie Sullivan was sitting at the same table they had frequented the day before. His bald chrome doom was prominent. He was wearing a dark, zip-up jacket. He seemed a lot bulkier in dark, as if the shade emphasised his wide thick chest and barrel shape. Moseley realised he hardly knew Sullivan. Something in the back of his mind told him he might have been somehow involved in all this.

But what? He wasn't exactly sure, nevertheless something told him he might have had a hand in this somewhere along the line. There were tell-tale signs. Like the time when they had arrived at the stables. Sullivan had led the way along the path to the side of the racetrack. Maybe he had been there before, or was it that he just guessed which path to take.

As Moseley entered the pub, Sullivan turned to look up at him, then he raised his hand that contained a glass with an amber liquid. Moseley joined him at the table so they were sat across the pine top. The waxy leaves of a rubber plant in a glass pot were gently wafting by the force of the draught from the ceiling fan.

Within moments of settling into the seat a pretty waitress was making her way to the table to hand Moseley a menu for lunch and to take his order. A bowl of steaming hot onion soup with croutons wouldn't go amiss.

Sullivan had dark lines under his eyes as if he hadn't had much sleep the night before. He eyed Moseley with a neutral expression etched on his face.

"How's it going?" he asked.

Moseley sat back in the seat. "Not good," he replied as he continued to run his eyes over the menu. He asked the waitress for a bottle of lager, but changed his mind about the soup, ordering a chicken curry with rice, instead. She took his order then left them alone.

"What's not good?" Sullivan enquired as soon as she had gone.

"Someone breaking into my hotel room. That's not good," Moseley said.

"Oh, my God," was Sullivan's somewhat over-played reply. He ran a hand over the top of his forehead as if he was patting down a non-existent hair piece. "What happened?"

"I returned to the hotel last night to discover someone had broken in and rifled through my things," Moseley replied.

"Did they take anything?" he asked.

Moseley was instantly aware that he had used the word 'they' as if he knew more than one person was involved. "Nothing," he replied. "The safe was still intact."

"Maybe they were disturbed," said Sullivan. There it was again. The word 'they'.

In the next moment, the waitress was at Moseley's side with an open bottle of lager in one hand and a glass in the other. She placed the bottle and the glass onto the table top. "Your food will be two minute," she said, then stepped back towards the bar.

"What time was this?" Sullivan asked.

"About eight o'clock."

"Where'd you been?" Sullivan enquired.

Moseley wondered why he wanted to know. "To the racetrack," he replied. Above him the speed of the fans suddenly increased so the waft of breeze became stronger.

"So, nothing was taken?" Sullivan asked.

"Nothing."

"They must have been opportunists."

Again, the plural rather than the singular. Moseley poured the contents of the bottle into the glass. He looked at the label. It was a well-known imported brand. A bit like Sullivan. He had been in Hong Kong for much longer than the imported product. He knew a lot of prominent people from his days in the police department. He must have accumulated quite a few associates and friends in all his years on the island. In this time, he must have also accumulated quite a few people who disliked him.

Moseley took the glass and drank a mouthful of the amber liquid. It had quite a bitter tangy taste that left a hit on the back of his throat, almost as if it had been in the bottle for too long. He looked at Sullivan who took a long sip of beer before raising his head and looking at him.

"Do you have any idea who broke into your room?" Sullivan asked.

"No."

"Strange isn't it that someone would want to break in. Maybe they were searching for something."

"Like what?" Moseley asked.

"Tell me this."

"What?"

"Who knows you're here in HK?"

"Ho Fung, you and Leo Sinnott," Moseley replied.

"Plus, the people in the hotel and the people you booked the trip with."

"That's true," said Moseley. He took a good intake of the lager. A taste of bitter almond once again nipped the back of his tongue. He looked at the glass in his hand, then at Sullivan whose face began to contort and become almost like a gargoyle caricature. Moseley tipped his head back as he tried to dislodge the image from in front of his eyes. He looked up to the ceiling and the blades of the fan turning above his head. Then he suddenly felt ill and with that feeling a misty haze seemed to fall in front of him and double vision played in his eyes. The four blades of the fan emerged and became one spinning arm. The strength of the chatter near to him came and went in decreasing then increasing echoing waves. His head suddenly began to feel heavy and he had a sensation of being on the edge of a precipice. The glass slipped from his hand and hit the table top, shattering into several pieces. The liquid spilled over the pine surface. Before he knew what was happening his whole body seemed to go into convulsions. His hands went into spasm. Noises in the distance seemed to echo and increase three-fold in decibels. He tried to focus his eyes on Sullivan's face and say 'what the fuck' but the words came out as a slurring undecipherable garble. Then a darkness fell and he slumped forward onto the table head first as his lights went out.

Moseley lifted his head. His neck felt stiff. He opened his eyes and cringed against a bright, brilliant yellow light beaming into his eyes. He felt as if his whole body was spinning like a Catherine wheel. He could taste the scent of vomit in his mouth. After a few moments of consciousness, he realised his wrists were secured to the arms of a chair by duct tape wrapped around his wrists. He was fixed to the arms of a chair.

Beyond, in the brilliant blinding light he could just about make out the dark shape of a figure sitting at the other end of a table. The air was stone cold and there was a dust filled, fusty smell in the air. The light was so blinding he couldn't keep his eyes open for a few seconds before he had to close them. He felt an ache in his stomach and the remaining scent of nausea in his throat. He tried to move his arms, but they were well and truly secured to the chair armrests. He could feel the rungs of the chair grating into his buttocks and the edge of the seat cutting into the back of his knees. The room was pitch black. He was aware for the first time that he was naked, but for his underwear.

"Moseley," said a voice from in front of him. The sound pinged against the solid concrete walls of the cell or the dungeon. There were no windows or any outside light.

"Who sent you to Hong Kong?" the voice asked. The accent was oriental English.

"Ho Fung," he replied.

"Why?"

"Why? What?" Moseley asked.

"Why you come here?"

"To find Lily Fung."

"Why does he want to find her?"

"I don't know."

"When you find her. What then?"

"I'm to take her back to London with me."

"Why does he want her to return?" the voice asked.

"I don't know. He never told me."

"How do you know she wants to go back with you?"

"I don't," said Moseley. It dawned on him that the mysterious person before him may know where she was. "Where is she?" he asked.

The silhouette figure did not reply. Moseley felt he was slowly returning to some form of normality, though he didn't recognise the voice of the interrogator. With the blinding white light, he couldn't see him, only the outline of his head. He could hear his voice. From the accent and tone, he guessed the man was Hong Kong Chinese and he was in his fifties or sixties. He tried to move his hands to loosen the tape around his wrists. It was a pointless exercise. He wasn't going to be able to free his hands anytime soon.

"You come here to find the wife of Hue Fung?" the voice asked. "And did you?"

"No."

"You know nothing. You mission, it failed," the man said and laughed out loud. The sound bounced against the thick side walls.

Moseley was suddenly aware there was another person at his back. He looked over his left shoulder. The figure emerged out of the dark. He was a man, dressed from head to toe in black. He had black-lens sunglasses over his eyes and a black cap on his head. He stepped to Moseley's left side and proceeded to tie a thin leather strap around his bicep, then pulled it tight. He held a syringe in his hand. The applicator was open and there was a colourless substance inside the transparent tube. The needle must have been six centimetres long and had a tip as sharp as a hat pin. The man twisted the strap. Under the pressure, a vein in his bicep popped up. The man prodded the tip of the needle into his flesh, punctured the skin, applied pressure to the applicator and emptied the content of the syringe into Moseley's blood.

Chapter 9

Weird dreams filled with spinning wheels, a kaleidoscope of assorted colours and shapes and a cacophony of different sounds filled Moseley's brain. A dry ice mist swirled in front of his vision. He could see himself in a kind of outer body experience as he rolled and tumbled down a steep decline and into a dark pit of a concrete-lined bunker.

His eyes flickered open. He could make out a dark shape above him. He was in the land of the living, or maybe this was death, part of a dream sequence or a near death experience. Nonetheless, the first feelings of consciousness were returning to him and he calculated he was back in the real world, if such a thing existed.

As he returned to the here and now his eyes focused. The dark shape above him was a ceiling. During the course of the next ten seconds he became aware of his surroundings. He was laid flat with a cushioned surface beneath him. He could taste the remnants of vomit in his mouth, feel a sticky salt like dryness in his throat and a fragrant smell at his nostrils. He lifted his right hand and rubbed it across his mouth. He could feel the thick bristle of stubble on his chin and along his jawline. A pain throbbed in his head and there was an ache in his legs. He felt as if he was in the eye of thc worst alcohol-induced hangover he had ever experienced in his life. He closed his eyes, then opened them again and saw double vision that sent his head spinning like an out-of-control child's spinning top.

His head continued to throb and a cloud of mist still remained in his eyes. He closed them then opened them again before managing to turn his head to observe a white lace curtain fluttering by an open window. He could feel the force of a light breeze blowing across his face. The backdrop of a blue sky was highlighted against the window frame. It took him a few seconds to realise he was laid on a mattress of a bed with a linen sheet beneath him. His head was deep in the softness of a sponge pillow. Above him was a timber panel roof that met in the centre directly above his head to form the apex of a structure.

He was totally naked. Then on his upper left arm he was aware of a weight pressing down on that side of the mattress. He instinctively turned his head in that direction in a series of robotic-like movements. When he came face-to-face with what was on the other side of the mattress it stunned him to the core of his soul. He found himself looking into the sickly pale blanched face of a woman. Her eyes were closed. She could have been sleeping, but there were no sounds coming from her. All sound had gone from her being. Her dry lips were a shade of cornflower blue. A wedge of dark hair had fallen across her forehead. She wore a pale mask of death.

He tried to pull himself up and summon the strength to lift the top half of his frame into an upright position. It took a huge amount of effort before he managed to raise his head off the pillow. Then a dizziness came over him and hurt his eyes. He had to lower himself back down into the softness of the pillow.

Several moments passed then he attempted to get up for a second time. Again, it took an enormous effort. On this occasion he was able to move his legs and swing them around ninety degrees so he was sitting on the edge of the mattress. Out of the window the view was of a tree-lined terrace sweeping up a steep hillside possibly a mile or so into the distance. Buildings were perched on the hillside at varying levels. In the background the cry of a flock of seagulls was audible against the sound of the sea rolling in over a beach or rocks somewhere close by. As if to emphasise he was near to the sea he could taste salt particles on his lips. He remained sitting on the bed for a while to let his senses return to something resembling normal. He was still finding it difficult to focus his eyes and collect his thoughts into a coherent order. No matter, he knew he had to get out of this place. There was a dead woman lying on the other side of the mattress. Then he wondered if his captors were close by. He stayed perfectly still for the next thirty seconds and listened for any sounds. He couldn't hear anything except for the cry of the gulls and the swoosh of the waves lapping onto a near-by beach.

His clothing was scattered over the floor. As he had no memory he couldn't recall ever being in this room, then the scene in the cell with the piercing white light came back into his mind. He saw the darkened image of the guy injecting the contents of a syringe into his arm. He asked himself how long he had been out.

With a determined thrust from his thighs he was able to get to his feet and stand erect. He moved forward a few paces to the window and peered out. He was raised up from the ground, maybe fifteen feet or so above a grassy terrain. Directly below was a narrow semi-rough track that led to a rocky beach approximately fifty yards away. He turned his head back to look at the mattress and the dead body. She was naked. Her legs were tightly clamped together. Then he saw the table at the other side of the bed and the items on it. He concentrated his sight on it. There was a glass bong, a thin leather strap, a large silver metal dessert spoon, tinfoil, a syringe, a cheap gas-filled cigarette lighter and a plate that had a heap of white powder on it. Everything a heroin addict needed to score.

He looked at the face of the woman. She looked familiar, but he didn't know where he had seen her before. It took him a good fifteen seconds to see it was the face of the woman in the photograph. Had he found Lily Fung?

He gingerly stepped over the rough wood floor to the other side of the bed frame, leaned over the body and looked at her. She had the same long raven hair, the same slim face. The same skinny slender frame. It was her. He had found her. Sadly, she wouldn't be going home with him.

He murmured the word *'fuck'* to himself. After a few moments he went to the other side of the bed, and picked up the items of his discarded clothing.

He still felt very dizzy, unsteady on his feet and in a kind of daze. Nonetheless, he was able to put his clothes on. His watch was in his jacket pocket along with some money. Maybe fifty dollars in notes and some loose change. The time on his watch said six-forty-five. He guessed it was the morning as the sun was low in the sky.

He dressed himself as best as he could, then went back to the body and examined it by checking her arms. There was a track of pinpricks in the fleshy part of her upper left arm. Someone must have injected her or she had done it herself. She may have passed-away due to a heroin overdose. Though there was no telling. He guessed the white powder on the plate was heroin. He must have also been injected with the same chemical but couldn't be sure. Had he survived an overdose or hadn't been injected with enough to kill him. He didn't know. What he did know was that he had to get away from here as soon as possible. Despite feeling like death, he felt his cognizance returning to him in small doses. He went to the window and peered out again. He could just make out the roofs of a settlement perhaps a quarter of a mile away snaking up the side of the hillside with its jungle-like terrain. Out over the ocean a junk was drifting across the sea. There was nothing else to see except for the horizon which suggested to him he may have been on the remote side of Hong Kong island. Maybe he was miles from Hong Kong. For all he knew he could be on the Chinese mainland.

He put the curtain to a side, put his head out of the window, sucked in a deep intake of fresh air, then ran a finger over his upper left arm. He could feel a sore welt on his flesh where a needle had penetrated the skin. It looked and felt red, almost like the aftermath of a bee sting. Maybe he was supposed to wake-up from the sleep and find her or maybe he wasn't supposed to survive so they would be found dead together, the result of a heroin overdose.

Her mouth was slightly ajar as if she had taken one last deep breath before she expired. The look on her face was one of peace and deliverance from evil.

He took a few steps across the floor towards a closed door. There was still a massive throb in his head and a pain in his temple. Despite the wobbling effect in his legs he was able to grab the door handle, pull it and open the door. The opening led onto a landing then a dozen or so steep wooden steps of a flimsy stairway leading to a door at the bottom. The door had panes of frosted glass in it. He stepped onto the landing and took a firm hold of a rickety handrail. Before taking the first downward step he stalled to prick his ears and listen for any sound coming from inside the building. He couldn't hear a thing. After about twenty seconds he began the descent to the door at the bottom at a slow careful pace.

At the bottom of the stairs was a door on the right that might have led into a ground-floor space. He made it down the last few steps to the bottom, took a pace to his right, took the handle and pushed the door open. It opened into a shade-filled room that contained all sorts of junk like a rowing boat and various bits of fishing gear, such as nets, buoys, tarpaulin sheets, ropes and other gear. The building must have been a fisherman's store of some description. There was even a bicycle propped up against the side.

He gingerly moved inside the room and felt a thick layer of dust under his feet. It seemed as if no one had been in here for a very long time. A slant of sunlight was blazing through a crack running down the centre of a double wooden door to illuminate a cloud of dust particles. All was quiet and still. The sound of the sea rushing onto the shore just beyond the building was audible in the background. He knocked against a rusty oil can which fell to the floor and made a metallic clatter that rung in his ears like the chimes of a church bell.

He had clearly regained most of his senses, but he felt as if he was about to vomit at any time. He looked at the bicycle. It was perhaps thirty years old, but it still looked useable and roadworthy, although the tyres were flat to the rims. It might come in handy to help him balance so he took hold of the handlebar and manoeuvred it across the floor and out through the door.

Once at the outer door he took the handle, pushed on it and the door opened. As it did a wave of fresh air rushed inside and he breathed it in, then he coughed several times as a sheet of dust particles went up his nostrils and lay on his throat.

Taking a tight grip of the bicycle he bowled it out of the door, up a five feet wide incline and onto the dirt track. Overhead, he was aware of the warmth of the early morning and the sound of seagulls sitting on the roof of the building and calling out. He looked up the side to see the white cotton curtain billowing out of the window of the room he had just left. It still didn't seem like this was happening, almost as if he was stuck in some kind of never-ending dream or a scene in some weird arthouse movie. This was the real world.

He stayed motionless for a few moments and contemplated his next move. He had to discover where he was, then try and get back into the city. Then he realised he had to do something. He placed the bicycle on the ground then went back inside the building and climbed the stairs to the room. He went inside. First, he took the sheet on the mattress, pulled it out from underneath her body and laid it over her. He wanted to give her some dignity in death, then his eyes went to the white powder and the syringe. He decided to do something for a reason he wasn't sure. He took the spoon. There was a trace of powder in the base. The underside was blackened by the flame from the lighter. He put the spoon into the powder, scooped up a heaped level, then took the lighter, flicked on the flame and began to turn the powder into a liquid. Next, he took the syringe. There was a small amount of red liquid in the tube. It must have been blood. He pressed down on the applicator to eject it. Then he put the needle into the fresh liquid and drew it into the tube. He filled it half-full, then he put the syringe into the inside pocket of his jacket.

He had one last look around the room, then he went out onto the landing, down the steps, carefully one at a time, and out into the daylight.

Picking up the bicycle by the handlebars he pushed it up the slight incline and onto the dirt track. After walking for twenty yards towards a spread of buildings in the distance he paused to take a breather and look back to the ramshackle building he had left behind. Beyond, the flat, calm surface of the sea stretched away to the horizon. The vessel he had observed must have laid anchor as it didn't appear to be moving against the backdrop of the green and blue horizon.

He turned back and held the handlebars tightly to aid his balance. The feeling of sick in his throat had reduced and the foggy blurring of objects and the sensation of dizziness were going, but he still felt as if he was wading through treacle.

The whole episode he had just witnessed was like the component parts of a bad dream. What he didn't know was how the dream ended or for how long it lasted. By the feeling of the stubble on his face he had been out for at least two days. Could it be that he had lain on that bed for over forty hours or even longer? By the rumbling in his stomach the answer to that was probably yes.

He continued up the incline of the dirt track for about two hundred yards then came across a tarmac road that led towards the buildings in a small settlement. He didn't have a clue where he was. He doubted he was in mainland China. After all, there was a controlled border between the New Territories and Shenzhen he would have to cross. What he did know was that he had to get away from here. With every passing stride his thoughts were becoming a little bit more coherent.

Chapter 10

After walking for five minutes, he was close to the end of the track and the nearest buildings came into sharper focus. Up ahead was a road, then a car appeared and swept by. By the fact that the vehicle was on the left-hand side of the road he knew he was still on Hong Kong island.

On reaching the end of the track he turned onto the tarmac road. There was a road-sign further ahead which pointed in the direction of Stanley, therefore he knew he was on the south side of the island. As the atoll was thirty-four square miles in area it was only about four or five miles back to the area of Wanchai and the centre of the city.

As the warm air wafted over him, he could feel his body returning to some form of normality, though he still had a throbbing ache in his forehead and down both temples. He progressed along the road and edged towards the fringe of a tiny settlement of no more than a dozen structures. He still had hold of the handlebars of the bicycle. Up ahead were the high peaks of the hillsides that effectively split the island in two. He didn't intend to walk all the way back into town.

After another one hundred yards he was in the settlement of small, mostly modest, unassuming houses. Further along the road was a bus-stop and an adjoining shelter. He slowly made it up the road to the centre, then leant the bicycle against a brick and mortar wall and took a few steps to the bus-stop. A couple of local people: a youth and an elderly lady were standing inside the metal shelter waiting for a bus. They observed him. He smiled which didn't draw a reaction. He must have looked like a vagrant. His hair was dishevelled and the growth of bristles on his chin and jawline must have given him the appearance of someone who had been partying for too long.

He put his eyes on the youth. The chap was pleasantly dressed in jeans and a t-shirt under a tight denim jacket. He wore round-rimmed wire spectacles over his eyes and had the strap of a rucksack perched over one shoulder.

"Excuse me," said Moseley. "Do you speak English?"

The guy's languid look appeared to stiffen. "I speak a little," he replied.

"Is there a bus which goes into Wanchai?"

"Wanchai?"

"Yes."

"The number *tree*," he said and looked up to the plate on top of the pole. "In ten minute from now," he said.

Moseley thanked him. He took a step back and leaned against the Perspex sheet at the back of the hut. Feeling in his jacket pocket he took the few notes and the handful of loose change. At least he had the fare to get into Wanchai. He could also feel the weight of the syringe in his breast pocket.

A single-deck, blue and yellow Hong Kong transport mini-bus, arrived a minute or two after the scheduled leave time. Moseley got on after the elderly lady and the youth, gave the driver some of the coins, and took a seat close to the front. There were only five people on the bus as it set off for the city. It wasn't long before it was grinding up the first of the hillsides that form the spectacular backbone of the island.

After a struggle it managed to ascend to the top of the peak, and the full eight-mile-long spread of the north side of the island appeared below in the valley that sloped down to the harbour. It was indeed one of the truly breath-taking sights with the multitude of skyscrapers and huge office towers reaching skyward and the spread of green topped hilltops disappearing into the distance.

The bus took the quick route into town along the main Wanchai road. Within twenty minutes of setting out the grandstands of Happy Valley racetrack and the line of apartment blocks in Leighton Hill came into view.

The morning sun was just beginning to slip behind some cloud, but the prospect of a warm day was on the cards. The tops of the glass and steel in the tower blocks in the central district were already gleaming bright.

Moseley wondered what to do. Whether to make the hotel his first port of call to take a shower and change his clothes. He didn't know if that was such a good idea. Maybe someone in the hotel was connected to this. Was Mr Lee a player? Could it have been Mr Lee, or his accomplice, who had entered his room to look for evidence of his mission. On that note he decided to hold-fire on returning to the hotel until much later in the day. Then he began to think about the sequence of events that had got him to this point in his investigation. Had he survived an attempt to kill him? Was he supposed to be found dead with Lily Fung in a conspiracy linked to her death? He didn't know the answer to either of those questions. It left him feeling tormented to a degree. He felt relatively okay in himself and relieved he was still breathing, but at the same time beaten and abused by those who had killed Lily and those who had possibly attempted to frame him for her murder.

As the bus came close to the racecourse it stopped at a bus stop to pick up several passengers. Moseley had an idea. He knew he was fairly close to Leo Sinnott's home. Perhaps he should pay him a visit. He got up from his seat and stepped off the bus. From here he crossed the road and ambled along the pavement adjacent to the back of the racecourse grandstands. The area of Leighton Hill was perhaps half a mile away. He knew there was a long flight of stairs to climb then he would be on the hilltop overlooking the racetrack.

As he walked, he ran his hand over his head. The heat of the sun was already beginning to make itself felt, though it wasn't much past eight o'clock. The traffic on the road wasn't heavy, therefore he assumed it was Saturday or Sunday morning. Had he really been out of it for more than forty hours? By the thickness of the bristles on his chin and the smell of perspiration coming from him it may have been that long. The effect of the chemical in his bloodstream was giving him the occasional hot flush on his skin and a slight blurring of his vision. Still it wasn't as bad as it had been an hour before.

It took him the best part of the next thirty minutes to ascend a long concrete staircase to reach the top of the hill overlooking the racecourse and the spread of the city beyond. Above him the eight-tower complex of Leighton Hill loomed high. The green-turquoise sun blinds in the balcony windows beamed out from the face and resembled blocks of exotic jade stone. He had no idea if Sinnott would be at home or even in town. The only way to find out was to enter the tower, ride up to the thirtieth-fifth floor and knock on the door to his apartment. The only way he could gain entry to the building was through the gate leading into the ground floor car park.

When he had arrived in Sinnott's vehicle, the first thing he noticed was the security camera by the left side of the gate, which meant there was a blind spot on the other side. If he could sneak through on the right side, as a vehicle entered or left the car park, then he might be able to gain access without been seen. It was in many ways trial and error. If he did gain entry and confront Leo it would be interesting to see how he reacted to his appearance. If he was involved in the murder of Lily Fung, he might choose to admit it. Or alternatively he might deny having anything to do with her death. Moseley knew he would have to play it cute. He couldn't be one hundred per cent sure that the body was that of Lily Fung. He had to assume it was. The only other possibility was that it was someone who looked very much like her.

On reflection, he wondered if he should have alerted the police or gone straight to his hotel to shower, rest, change into a fresh set of clothes and consider what his best strategy should be. Too late. He was close to the glass foyer entrance of tower C.

As there were a lot of apartments in the tower, he assumed it would only be a matter of time before a car approached and stopped at the gate.

He followed a path by the service road and came to the back of the tower. A wide wedge of shadow from the structure was projected out over the grassed area which was festooned with patches of flower beds and the occasional park bench. At a point where the block C began, he crossed the road and approached the gate in the wall.

There were several huge support columns that jutted out from the building so he would be able to hide from view in the shadows. He couldn't see any other cameras attached to the structure.

He edged towards the turn off in the road that led to the gate. A white painted sign above the opening read: 'Car park entrance' and the equivalent in Cantonese characters. There was a continuous steel mesh fence that prevented anyone from gaining access into the car park. He was aware of the sound of a car inside the car park. He was just too late as the car appeared and came out of the opening. The heavy metal gate rolled down and closed over the entrance.

An opportunity missed. Never mind he would be patient and wait for the next opportunity.

He stayed out of view by standing in the shadows and hidden behind one of the columns. Though he was in the shadow if a car came along the road and slowed to turn, the driver would surely see him. Ten minutes passed. Ten minutes became twenty. No vehicles came along. A further ten minutes ticked by. He was starting to feel a little conspicuous, but still no one had spotted him. Standing in the shade he was beginning to feel chilly but couldn't do anything other than shiver and close the buttons on his jacket.

It wasn't too long before he heard an approaching car on the service road. The engine noise reduced as the speed decreased. The car turned into the short road leading to the roll-up gate. He set himself to dart behind the body as it pulled up by the gate. He chanced a quick glance at the car. It was a long, sleek black saloon. A single driver in the car. The vehicle went out of view. Nevertheless, he could hear a metal rattle of the gate lifting and the sound of the hydraulic motor echoing inside the cavernous area.

He edged forward to take a peek around the corner. The car was just about to drive under the rolled-up gate. In the same instant the sound of the motor ceased and the car moved into the gap. Moseley stepped out from the shadow, crouched down and got close to the back end of the car and slipped through the opening as the vehicle went inside the car park.

The car drove off into the interior and the screech of brakes echoed around the roof like the squeal of a frightened animal. Moseley slipped by the inner wall and looked into the shade, at the parked cars, each in their own allocated bay. The block that contained the lifts was approximately forty yards away. After a moment to acclimatise, he made his way in between two cars, crossed the floor, and went to the lift doors.

He couldn't see any security cameras. He soon made it to the lift doors and pressed the call button. It was a minute before the car arrived at the floor. There was a ping as it reached the ground floor. The car wasn't empty. It contained two people, an elderly man and woman. They didn't look surprised to see him standing there. He smiled and said 'good morning' then stood aside to let them pass. He stepped into the car, faced the control panel, and pressed the button with the number 'thirty-five' on it.

From what he could recall from the visit with Sullivan there were no CCTV cameras on the landing. The lift quickly accelerated up the building. Within a matter of thirty seconds the car was slowing down as it neared the thirty-fifth floor.

As the door slid open, he peered out and onto the landing with its red and burgundy circular pattern carpet and mauve paint walls. The walls were lined with silver-framed picture frames, he hadn't noticed the first time, all at equal length along the corridor. He turned to the right and walked down the corridor at a relaxed pace. Each of the frames had a photograph of an iconic Hong Kong scene behind a sheet of thin glass. There was no one in the corridor and no sound; not even his feet as they sank into the lush pile.

Chapter 11

Moseley was soon outside the door to apartment 35A. He pressed the doorbell. After thirty seconds no one had come. He pressed the button for a second time. Maybe Sinnott wasn't at home. No problem. He would wait for him to return, but then he could hear a key turning and a bolt opening. The door opened to a narrow degree and a face appeared in the gap. It took him a few moments to see it was Leo Sinnott. The thick metal links of a security chain were stretched across the opening. Leo looked half sleep as if Moseley had just got him out of bed. Behind him the light inside the apartment had him framed in a kind of halo effect. He rubbed his eyes and blinked several times. He recognised Moseley.

"What you want?" he asked in a brusque tone.

"To talk."

"About what?" Sinnott asked.

"Why don't you open the door and let me in."

Sinnott could see Moseley was about to put his shoulder to the door and ram it. Rather than have him barge his way in and damage the door, Sinnott wisely elected to unhook the chain and open the door wide.

He was wearing a knee length, blue, silk man's kimono. His feet and legs were bare and the thick cover of black hairs on his chest was visible. Moseley had indeed got him out of bed. His hair was dishevelled, he was unshaven and there were sleep residues in his eyes. He didn't appear to be overly concerned by Moseley's sudden and unannounced visit to his home.

Just then there was the sound of a female voice from inside the apartment, asking or saying something in Cantonese. Moseley stepped in beyond the door and glanced to his right to see a pretty, long-legged girl appear in the doorway to the main bedroom. She was wearing a man's button-down shirt which came level to the centre of her thighs. She saw Moseley, stared at him for a few fleeting moments, then turned into the bedroom and went out of view.

Leo said something in Cantonese, but remained calm and unperturbed. He tightened the sash around the kimono and pulled it tight to his waist.

"What you want?" he asked for a second time.

"I think you know."

Sinnott's face rippled into a quizzical frown. "Know what?" he asked.

"That Lily Fung is dead."

Sinnott took a step back. His expression changed from one of puzzlement to one of stunned surprise. "Lily?" he exclaimed. "How?"

"You tell me," Moseley said.

"Tell you what?"

"How she died."

"I don't know," he said adamantly. Though it was early in the exchange his body language and reaction seemed to suggest he may have been telling the truth.

Moseley moved into the centre of the lounge and looked out of the window to the spread of the undulating cityscape in the near distance. He put his eyes back on Sinnott who was patting his hair down, but hadn't moved from the spot close to the door. "She died from a drug overdose," Moseley said and gauged Sinnott's reaction, which was closed. "Someone filled her blood with a chemical that popped her heart. They've tried to make it look like an overdose."

"Who are they?" Sinnott asked, seemingly dumfounded by the tragic turn of events. He was assuming that more than one person was involved. In this case he was probably on the money.

Moseley looked at him. "I've no idea who *they* are," he said. "But you might."

Sinnott stared at him with a startled expression. "No way," he snapped. His use of slang made his denial sound slightly more authentic.

"What did she know?" Moseley asked.

"About what?"

"Let's try the horse racing game for starters."

Sinnott looked perplexed and shook his head. "What're you getting at?" he asked, then took a few steps back across the hardwood floor in his bare feet.

"Did she know that Ho Fung was doping his race horses?"

"Doping horses?" he asked incredulously.

"Or is Fung using a performance enhancing cocktail. She knew this and threatened to reveal the practice." It was a theory Moseley had considered, but he didn't have a shred of evidence if it was anywhere near the truth.

Sinnott looked genuinely stunned by the allegation. "I've no idea what you're talking about," he replied in a stiff tone.

Moseley took a step to a side and put his hands on the edge of the circular sofa. Sinnott remained standing in a defensive posture with his legs wide and his arms down by his side. He looked less tall and much less flash in bedroom attire.

"Is Fung using performance-enhancing steroids?" Moseley asked. "Did she know and threatened to tell? Therefore, he paid you to seduce her to bring her back here so he could have her silenced. Then he sent me to look for her to act all innocent."

Sinnott took in his words and the underlining theory. "That's crazy," he said.

"It's a possibility," said Moseley.

"But it's not true."

"How are you so sure?"

Sinnott didn't answer. There was a period of silence that lasted twenty seconds while they both took stock of the situation. "How are you absolutely sure she's dead?" Sinnott asked, voicing a modicum of concern in the tone.

"I've seen her body," Moseley replied.

"Where?"

"In a place on the other side of the island."

"Whereabouts?"

"In a small abandoned hut, near to Stanley," replied Moseley. He looked to the window as the sun appeared at the edge of a dark cloud to produce an array of golden sunrays that spread far and wide over the city like a blast of power from several klieg spotlights.

"Take me to the place," Sinnott said.

"Why?"

"I want to see her."

"It's not a pretty sight."

"I need to know she's dead and it's her."

Moseley wondered why he was so adamant. Maybe he had a genuine desire to see her with his own eyes. "Why would you want to do that?" he asked.

"I feel as if I'm guilty for her death," said Sinnott. "I need to know you're telling me the truth," he added.

"Okay. Fine. If you insist. Let's go. I'll take you to where she is," Moseley said. He was in effect calling his bluff. Maybe Sinnott had no idea Lily Fung was dead or perhaps he was wiser than he acted. Moseley knew he wasn't to take him lightly. Sinnott was shrewd. He had to keep his guard all the time.

Sinnott asked to be excused for a minute. He stepped into the bedroom; through the door the girl had emerged from. Moseley could hear them talking in a hushed tone. He remained by the edge of the sofa, listening to the conversation, but he couldn't understand a word. The effect of the drug in his system had all but gone from his body. Climbing the steep concrete staircase from the base of the valley to the garden in front of the apartment block could have sweated out most of the residues of the chemical. He could feel damp under his armpits and in the nooks and crannies all over his body. He looked at his clothing, then felt the bristles above his top lip and along his jawline. He must have resembled a vagabond, but that was the least of his worries.

Sinnott came out of the bedroom. He was clipping the steel strap of a watch over his right wrist. He had changed into a pair of black gym trousers and a round neck red t-shirt which had a well-known designer's logo splashed across it. He had clearly dressed in haste. It appeared that he was keen for Moseley to take him to see the body of Lily Fung.

Moseley looked at him. "Tell me this?" he said.

"Tell you what?" asked Sinnott.

"What day is it today?"

Sinnott looked at him, bemused by the question. "It's Saturday," he replied.

"Geez. I've been out for nearly two days," Moseley said under his breath.

"Out of where?"

"My head…I was drugged for two whole days." Sinnott didn't reply. "Can I use your bathroom?" he asked.

Sinnott looked towards the door to the room. "Of course," he replied.

Moseley stepped through the door and inside the room with the black wall tiles, the sleek fittings and the gleaming white porcelain washbasin. The face that greeted him in the mirror was like that of a stranger. He hardly recognised himself. He looked like death warmed up. His face was thin and gaunt. His eyes looked like saucers stirring out of pale grey flesh. He hadn't eaten anything substantial for nearly two days. He hadn't shaved for three mornings so his face was beginning to develop a kind of hound-dog appearance. His clothing was dishevelled and dirty. His jacket and shirt were stained with sweat and dirt. He looked like a man who had slept rough for the past two days.

He slipped off the jacket and shirt, then ran hot water into the basin and washed his hands and face. Never in a million years had the effect of warm water hitting his skin felt so good.

Sinnott appeared in the frame of the door behind him. He had put on a casual zip-up sports jacket over the t-shirt. Moseley dried himself, slipped back into his shirt and jacket, then stepped into the lounge area to where Sinnott was standing by the long balcony window looking out over the spread of the city. Down below in the valley, Wanchai Road snaked around the racecourse and off into the distance. The huge grandstands and the oval area of open land in which the track stood were like a green oasis in a sea of concrete. Ironic, perhaps that Moseley assumed this whole affair might have had something to do with the doping of racehorses Ho Fung owned. Maybe it wasn't the correct assumption, but it was still one that resonated in his mind. There was one other person who may have known a great deal more about the why's and the what's of this affair and that was Laurie Sullivan. Moseley had to catch up with him.

As he came close to Sinnott he turned to face him. He had his car keys in his hand. "We go now?" he said as if he was eager to get out.

"Yeah."

Either he was playing a clever game or he was on the level. Either way Moseley had to keep his wits about him. He followed Sinnott across the lounge and they went out through the front door. The time was a shade after ten o'clock.

Once out on the corridor they went to the lift. No words were exchanged.

Within a matter of four minutes of leaving the apartment they were driving out of the ground floor car park in Sinnott's top-of-the-range 4x4.

He took the turn onto Wanchai Road and headed in a southerly direction. Moseley remained mute. He was eager to see if the playboy, race horse trainer would lead him to the ramshackle building without been given directions of where to go.

It was the reverse route the bus had taken slightly more than an hour before. Nothing was said. Sinnott concentrated on driving and drove at a reasonable pace towards the area near to Aberdeen harbour. Moseley wondered if he would drive straight to the fisherman's hut and therefore reveal he knew far more about the location than he was letting on. He decided to enact some conversation and seek to get more information out of him.

"You still have no idea why Ho Fung wanted her to return to England?" he asked Sinnott.

"No," His one-word answer was given in a blunt tone.

"And you've no idea where she may have been staying after she left your place?"

"No," he replied again. He had his eyes fixed on the road. They were now on a stretch of road several miles from Leighton Hill going down a narrow road that contained several blind corners and sharp bends that required full concentration. A line of vehicles was coming up the hill in the opposite direction. "When I accepted Fung's request to bring her to Hong Kong, I didn't know why. I didn't think it could lead to this," Sinnott volunteered.

"Lead to what?" Moseley asked.

"Her going missing."

"You were acting on his orders?"

"Yes."

"How much did he pay you?"

"Ten thousand pounds."

"Did you receive the money?"

"It was transferred into my London bank account."

"Ten thousand. Just to bring her here?"

"That's correct."

"Not a bad sum."

Sinnott didn't reply. He had his eyes on the road where it turned at a downhill S bend. "Now he desperately wants her back in London. I wonder why?" Moseley asked.

"No. I don't know," said Sinnott.

Moseley believed he was telling the truth. In a strange way he didn't think Sinnott was a bad person. Perhaps out of his depth. He was caught between a rock and a hard place. Moseley stayed silent and let him concentrate on driving.

Chapter 12

Within twenty minutes of setting out they were close to the turn off towards the town of Stanley with a view across the South China Sea where a scattering of tiny islands was spread out into the sea for as far as the eye could see. Aberdeen was on the western side, Stanley to the east. As they drove down the gradual decline from Violet Hill, they had a great view of the thick green-lined terraced hillsides, the flat calm of the sea and the armada of small fishing vessels close to the shoreline.

At the bottom of the hill the road forked off into two directions. Repulse Bay Road to the right and a stretch of road known locally as Island Road to the left.

"Which way is it?" Sinnott asked. Perhaps he sensed that Moseley was waiting for him to make a fatal mistake and lead him straight into the small town, then down the dirt track to the hut. Was he being cute? Moseley had no idea.

"Keep left," he replied.

"Island Road then," said Sinnott. Moseley didn't reply.

After another two minutes they were in the small town from where Moseley had caught the bus. The beach area and the turn off onto the dirt track was only another couple of hundred yards further along.

Sinnott slowed down as he went past the bus stop. The old rickety bicycle was still propped against the wall where Moseley had left it.

"Which way?" he asked.

"Drive on for another two hundred yards. There's a turn off on the right onto a dirt track that leads to a rocky cove and beach area."

Sinnott went through the town and down the incline. The turn off to the dirt track was only a matter of yards further on.

"There," said Moseley, pointing out the turn onto the track.

Sinnott reduced speed, waited for a car to pass on the other side of the road, then turned the wheels of the vehicle off the tarmac and swung the Nissan onto the rocky uneven terrain of the track. He manoeuvred slowly down the dirt road towards the beach area at the bottom of the hill.

The wooden structure was only a matter of two hundred yards further along the track. There were no other vehicles in sight and all appeared to be quiet. The road was so bumpy the chassis of the 4x4 rocked from side to side. It was on an incline that didn't seem to be this steep when he walked up it with the bike to help him keep his balance.

After another few yards the structure came into full view where the track levelled out and the land flattened to a narrow stretch of beach just beyond. The building was little more than a single, two storey structure that must have been an abandoned fisherman's store. As they came to it Moseley looked at the building. Something was missing, something didn't look right, but he couldn't put his finger on it for the moment.

"Is this the place?" Sinnott asked.

"This is the place," Moseley said. "Stop here."

"Here!" said Sinnott, as if he was crazy. "It's just an old storage hut for fishermen. No one will use it now," he said, as if he knew what he was talking about.

He pulled up outside and looked to the door with the glass panes in it.

"You certain?" he asked.

"Yeah," Moseley replied.

Moseley got out of the passenger side. He looked up to the side and noticed that the shutters over the open window were now closed. When he left, they were open. He stepped to the door and tried the handle. The door was still unlocked so he opened it and went inside where he was met by the stairway with the loose hand rail to a side. Sinnott was a couple of paces behind him.

The door to the ground floor storage room from where he had taken the bicycle was closed. Moseley could have sworn blind he had left it open when he had departed. He took the first step on the stairs and ascended up towards the room on the upper floor.

When he reached the landing at the top of the stairs, he looked into the room expecting to see the mattress and the body of Lily Fung covered with the white sheet. When he looked inside there was nothing. The room was completely empty.

The bed frame and the mattress were no longer there. There was nothing. No white sheet, no side table with the bong and the other drug-related items on it, no body of a naked female.

Moseley was stunned into silence. He turned back to see Sinnott enter the room and cast his eyes around the empty space.

"She was here, I tell you. In this room. Right there." He pointed to the spot where the bed had been. "She was lying on a bed right there. There was a table to the side, just there."

Sinnott raised his head and looked up into the roof to see speckles of light beaming through the tiny slits in the surface. "She's not here now," he said. "Perhaps you dreamt it all," he added in a what's-going-on tone.

"I tell you. She was…" Moseley's words tailed off. "Here I tell you," he said almost in a hush. He was at a loss to explain what had happened. In truth, there wasn't a lot to explain. Someone had come in, removed the body and took away the furniture and the other items.

Maybe she wasn't dead. Maybe he had dreamt it all. But then something caught his eye. He went to the shutter over the window. Something was moving in the draught. A piece of the lace curtain, several centimetres long, had become snagged on the end of a rusty nail. Whoever had removed the curtain had left a tiny ripped section remaining.

"Here. Look at this," Moseley said.

"What?"

"A piece of the curtain that was over the window."

Sinnott moved towards him and looked at what he was pointing at. "So?" he said.

“So, there was someone here. I haven’t dreamt anything,” snapped Moseley.

Just then there was a sound of the door at the bottom of the stairs coming open. This was instantly followed by the sound of feet on the stairs. In the next moment a figure appeared at the open door.

It was a man who looked to be in his mid to late fifties. He had the wizened face of a local fisherman. He was wearing a dirty sweatshirt with a faded motif on the front, baggy pants and a stained thin, red windcheater jacket. He had a plain baseball cap on his head with the peak pushed back so it was high on his head. Moseley noticed his hands were covered with dirt as if he had been clearing out items of furniture and the like.

As he came onto the landing, the man paused to eye the strangers inside the room, paying particular attention to Moseley. He glared at them in a disapproving fashion then said something to Sinnott in a volley of Cantonese.

“What’s he saying?” Moseley asked.

Sinnott didn’t reply. The two of them, Sinnott and the man, began to hold an animated conversation which quickly became heated.

“What’s he saying?” Moseley asked again.

Sinnott looked at Moseley, then suddenly in the blink of an eye his manner changed to a more assertive volatile one. He jumped towards Moseley and seemed to be reaching for something inside his jacket. Within an instant, he had extracted a shiny metal object which he held in a menacing fashion and assumed an offensive stance. He didn't say a word, then thrust his hand towards Moseley.

Moseley hardly had any time to comprehend what he had said or done. He reacted by taking a step backwards. In the same instant Sinnott raised his right-hand level with his shoulder and took another swing at him. A flash of steel in the form of the pointed end of a blade swished by him. Moseley managed to pull himself back at the moment of impact and narrowly avoided been stabbed high up on the chest. Meanwhile, the other fellow was moving on him from the other side in a coordinated harassing manoeuvre. Moseley instinctively assumed a defensive stance and raised his hands. He was trained in the art of self-defence, during his police training, therefore he wasn't going to be easily beaten into submission.

He sprang onto his tiptoes and stood there at a forty-five-degree angle, Sinnott to his right, the other guy on the left. A kind of standoff ensued with neither of them moving for a good five seconds. Moseley could feel adrenalin pumping into his veins. His whole body was now on high alert. It was then that he felt the weight of the syringe in his breast pocket. In the next second Sinnott moved a step forward and swung his hand again. Moseley anticipated the attack. He was able to use his right hand to block the move, but also grab hold of his arm at a point close to his elbow, then bring his left hand around and chop down onto his exposed wrist. Sinnott lost his balance for a brief second. His clenched fist came open and a dagger fell from his hand. It hit the floor with a solid thud. Moseley retained a grip of his wrist. He was able to make a fist of his left hand and bring it arching around and punch Sinnott on the jaw, all within a time frame no longer than a couple of seconds.

The force of the punch snapped Sinnott's head back. He was jerked backwards for one step. In the same movement Moseley kicked the dagger and sent it spinning across the wood planks to the other side of the room.

The other fellow now moved closer towards Moseley, but he had apprehension glued to his face. This was going to be harder than he had anticipated. Moseley turned slightly towards him, and aimed a kick. The sharp end of his foot caught him high up on the thigh and close to the groin. He was instantly doubled up with pain and shock. Reaching inside his breast pocket Moseley got hold of the syringe in his left hand. Sinnott looked dazed by the punch he had taken to the jaw, but he came back at Moseley. It was now one against one, fist against fist. The other one having sustained a kick was in no fit state to continue the fight.

Sinnott lunged at Moseley and attempted to grab hold of his front, but his movement was mistimed. He partly stumbled – partly hesitated in his approach. This, allowed Moseley to swing his left arm in a circular motion and thrust his hand towards the aggressor. He stabbed Sinnott with the needle of the syringe. The tip went deep into the right side of his neck at a point in or close to his carotid vein. Sinnott's immediate reaction was to put his hands to his neck and try to pull the needle out. But it was well and truly inserted into a bulging artery. In the act of swinging the syringe Moseley had pressed down on the applicator and injected most of the content into Sinnott.

His reaction was almost instantaneous. His eyes seemed to go cross-eyed and lose focus. His expression was one of dumfounded shock. Then his legs gave away and he fell to the floor with a thump. The needle still stuck into his neck.

On seeing that Sinnott was no longer able to fight, the other one attempted to leg it out of the room. Moseley ran after him and caught up with him on top of the landing. The fellow was about to take the first step down when Moseley got behind him. He raised his left foot, put it against his back, kicked out and sent him tumbling down the steps like a bag of bones turning over and over. He hit his head against the bottom of the bannister. Moseley took the handrail and went down the steps two at a time. The fellow wasn't moving and neither was he saying anything. He was knocked out cold. There was gash several inches wide on the top of his head from which blood was pouring.

Moseley turned back and went back up the stairs two at a time. Inside the room Sinnott was stretched across the floor. He was either dead, dying or in a drug-induced sleep. Moseley reached down, took his wrist and felt for a pulse. It was hardly registering. His heart may have already gone into cardiac arrest. His skin had taken on an almost blue-grey tinge. His limbs appeared to be limp. Moseley reached down, took the syringe and yanked it out of his neck. As he did a spurt of blood came out and splattered across the floor. The needle had gone straight into his carotid vein.

The milky-white colour of the heroin inside the tube had been replaced by a quantity of Sinnott's blood. Carefully and without touching the needle Moseley slipped the syringe back into his jacket breast pocket. He searched in Sinnott's jacket and found a wallet and the keys to his vehicle which he took into his possession.

With the car keys in his grip he left the room and went down the steps. He stepped over the crumpled heap of the guy at the bottom of the stairs, then went outside. He went to the 4x4, opened the door, climbed inside, got the motor running, put it into drive and drove along the dirt track and away from the wooden structure.

Chapter 13

Thirty minutes after setting out from the beach on the south side of the island, Moseley was driving along Wanchai Road and heading into the built-up area of central Hong Kong. He contemplated his next move. He toyed with the idea of heading to his hotel to pack his bag and get the hell out of Hong Kong. But was that such a good idea? His sudden reappearance at the hotel would reveal he was very much alive.

He had no idea if Sinnott and company had intended to kill him or just frighten him by knocking him out and leaving him next to a dead body. Could it be they sought to implicate him in the murder of the woman he was looking for. He had seen with his own eyes that Lily Fung was dead. Now he could give the sad news to Ho Fung. He asked himself if it was all part of a Fung family dispute. Like a lot of questions, he didn't know any of the answers. If it wasn't anything to do with a horse doping swindle, then it had to be something else.

Laurie Sullivan had to be involved in the affair in one capacity or another. After all, he must have been a willing player in drugging him with a form of Rohypnol, stripping him, then taking him to some place for interrogation before he was injected with heroin or whatever was in the syringe.

He had Sullivan's address from the last time he had been in Hong Kong. His landline telephone number hadn't changed therefore it was safe to assume he was still at the same address in Kowloon.

Sullivan's home was close to a sports stadium and in an area of Kowloon famed for its flower market. The last time he had been there was ten years ago. He didn't know how close it was for sure. After considering his options he decided to dump the vehicle somewhere in Central then take the Star Ferry across the harbour to Kowloon then a cab to the flower market area and find Sullivan's home.

He drove the 4x4 along the busy Hennessey Road, deep in the Central district and into an area that was in a valley of skyscrapers. The traffic was moving at a slow pace. After driving east for half a mile or so he saw the sign for a multi-story car park in a high-rise office and shopping complex. He drove off the main road, up a ramp and into a car park. He drove up several exterior circular ramps for five levels or so before he came across an empty space on the sixth floor of eight.

He parked the car. Before leaving he made sure to wipe his fingerprints off the steering wheel and the door handles. From here he made his way down six flights of stairs to the ground level and out onto the busy street. It took him five minutes to walk into the tightly packed business quarter, through an open-air clothes market and on towards the harbour front. On the way, he deposited the Nissan keys and Sinnott's wallet into a rubbish bin.

His plan was to take a Star ferry over to the Kowloon side of the harbour and seek out Laurie Sullivan's residence. He knew he lived in an address on Prince Edward Road. He vaguely recalled visiting his home. It was a tiny five room flat in a high-rise apartment block that must have been thirty years old even back then.

He soon made it to the harbour and the Star ferry terminal. It cost less than one pound to cross the iconic harbour to Shim Tsa Tsui on the Kowloon side. The quay area by the ferry terminal was close to the huge steel and glass structure of the Hong Kong convention centre. It was teeming with people, both locals and tourists alike. Each day seventy thousand people would cross the half mile wide harbour between the island and the land that was official termed as the 'New Territories'. It was perhaps one of the most sought-after short ferry trips on many people's bucket-list.

Moseley purchased a ticket from a coin-operated machine and boarded the next ferry along with several dozen passengers who were evenly spread between the upper deck and the lower deck. The boat soon set off over the choppy waters of the harbour for the ten-minute crossing to Shim Tsa Tsui.

On the Kowloon side of the harbour, adjacent to the famous Canton-Kowloon Railway clock tower, was an ornamental pond and garden. Tourists could purchase drinks from a number of vendors and linger to take photographs of the famous Hong Kong skyline from advantage points next to the promenade railings.

Moseley made straight for a nearby taxi rank. He had to wait five minutes for the next available cab. He asked the driver to take him to Prince Edward Road and the area near to the flower market.

Luckily for him the driver knew where he wanted to go. The taxi set off into the heart of bustling Kowloon with its busy streets, narrow pavements, and with its vast array of business signs. Air conditioning units hung out of windows in the almost never-ending stretch of tenement blocks set behind the street market stalls that line the length of Nathan Road.

After a journey of twenty minutes they were on a stretch of Prince Edward Road close to Mong Kok Stadium. Sullivan lived on the fifteenth floor of an apartment building near to the flower market and street side stall holders selling fruit and vegetables. Moseley recalled visiting him at home and admiring the excellent views over the stadium to the hillsides in the distance that marked the boundary between the New Territories and the beginning of the Chinese mainland. The city of Shenzhen skyline was visible in the haze.

Chapter 14

It wasn't that long before the taxi was in an area Moseley recognised. From memory he recalled the apartment block had a kind of narrow curved frontage with red paint edging to the stone of the façade. Eighteen floors high. He soon came across it on the western end of the road and close to the stadium.

Unlike ten years before, it was now hemmed in and dwarfed by a new slender condominium that was tightly squeezed in on one side. At ground level there was a long row of stores and stalls selling bushes, fledging trees and everything else associated with the horticulture trade. Roadside hawkers were stopping traffic on Prince Edward Road to sell posies of flowers to passing motorists.

Moseley asked the driver to stop on the corner where some steps went down to a concourse that led to turnstiles going into the stadium. He paid the fare, then got out and was immediately aware of the smell of freshly cut flowers and the sounds of this part of Kowloon. On the other side of the street, behind a line of shrubs was a chain link fence and the side of one of the stands of the sports stadium. Moseley wasn't sure which sports were played there. It may have been football, baseball, or rugby, or all three.

Before making a move, he watched the taxi pull away and disappear up the street, then he turned to walk the fifty yards to the front of the apartment block. There were four apartments on each floor – two at the front, two at the rear – making seventy-two in total. Each one had a small balcony. Air conditioning units were installed in the windows. Several of the balconies were festooned with tall plants. There was a sign on the front in Cantonese characters. The window frames looked in urgent need of replacement.

He was conscious of the need to find Sullivan quickly, but had no way of knowing if he was at home. He made his way across the path, up a step, through an open entrance and into a tight entrance. Flaking red and yellow masonry paint was peeling off the walls. The bottom half was red, the top was yellow. A notice in traditional Chinese characters and English asked the residents to ensure the front door was locked after nine at night. There was a stone clad stairwell doubling as a fire escape should the building catch fire. Straight ahead was a single lift shaft that served the entire building. He recalled using the lift when he had visited Sullivan all those years ago. From what he remembered his apartment was a compact space of five rooms that contained all the essentials for living. There wasn't a great deal of space, and very little in the way of storage, which wasn't uncommon in Kowloon. A balcony with the view across the border to Shenzhen was a bonus.

After a few moments to get his bearings he pressed the button to call the lift. The car came down from the third floor. He got in and pressed the button for the fourteenth floor. He would take the stairs for the final flight to the next floor.

The car was slow and rattled all the way up fourteen floors. Once there, he got out, opened a door to the stairwell and the stone steps serving the building. The stairwell was cold. A single pane window at the half-way turn allowed a shadowy insipid light to illuminate the otherwise dingy backdrop. He could feel his cold breath on his face. The sound of his feet against the stone chamber made a pinging echo.

When he reached the top of the stairs and the door that opened onto the fifteenth floor, he paused for a moment to listen for any sound. He couldn't hear anything except for the beat of his heart. He felt tense and jumpy. He gently opened the door, peered through then moved onto the corridor. A landing ran from one side of the building to the other, along a bare tile surface. There were two doors to flats across the corridor and opposite each other. Taking a step forward he gently closed the door, then moved onto the landing.

It was dim. Natural light was at a premium. Dull, and dusty bulbs attached to the ceiling provided the light, therefore the ends of the landing were bathed in permanent shadow. The space was narrow with hardly enough room for two people to pass. Sullivan's place was on the left, the last door facing the front of the building. He ventured forward. He could hear the sound of a voice from inside one of the flats or maybe it was from a television. He couldn't tell. This being Saturday afternoon, he assumed that many of the residents would be at work or in one of the public parks that dot this part of Kowloon. He made it down to the last door on the left-hand side. And there, attached to the door was a kind of decorative porcelain plate with the name of the flat owner: 'Laurie Sullivan,' engraved into it in dark paint letters.

He waited for a moment to collect his thoughts, steady himself, then he tapped on the door. He patted the breast pocket of his jacket to feel the shape of the syringe. No one came so he knocked for a second time, this time louder.

In the next moment he heard a chain being released from the door frame, then the sound of a bolt opening. As the door opened wider escaping sunlight raced across the landing. Moseley recognised Sullivan immediately. He was wearing jogging pants and an off-white sports type of string vest. Before Sullivan could utter a word, Moseley lunged at him and got the first punch in, hitting him plumb in the face. Sullivan staggered back through the doorway. Moseley followed him inside, stepped into an alcove and pushed Sullivan with a shove. He staggered back, fell through a metal ball-bearing curtain hanging from a door frame at the end of the alcove, and hit the deck with an almighty clatter. Moseley was soon upon him, wrapped his left hand around the vest to take a firm hold, and pummelled him in the face with a second punch.

Moseley stepped through the metal curtain and went into the living space. The room was tightly packed and scruffy. It must have been ten feet by twelve feet wide at most. There was a two-seater sofa on one side and a coffee table which was covered with several glossy, English-language magazines. A rug covered a plain tile floor. A paper lantern hung from the ceiling. The furniture was old and cheap. A kind of mix of Chinese reproductions and old country. On one wall were a couple of Monet prints of Westminster Bridge scenes at twilight or dusk. A retro, 1960s Manchester United football shirt was hanging on a coat hanger attached to a picture rail. A single door led onto the balcony with dusty looking windows allowing the daylight to illuminate the room. Behind the thin net curtain, it was just possible to make out the spread of rainbow-coloured seats in the stadium across the road.

Sullivan was on his back, but managed to get onto his haunches. He wasn't a young man and neither was he fit, but he was still a size and therefore a threat so Moseley was prepared to defend himself if Sullivan chose to come at him.

Sullivan shook his head as if he was trying to get the shock of the assault out of his system. He didn't utter a word, but he managed to spring to his feet and come swinging. Moseley anticipated an incoming punch, telegraphed it, and was able to duck out of the way. As Sullivan lunged his body Moseley twisted his knee and sent it slamming into his midriff. The blow propelled him back against the door leading onto the balcony. He fell to a side and onto the edge of the table which tipped over and sent the magazines flying into the air then spilling across the floor. It was only then that Moseley saw that a television was on. Sullivan had been watching a football game. The volume was so low it was hardly audible. He groaned out loud, managed to right himself and was about to get onto his feet when Moseley aimed a kick that hit him on the chin. The force propelled him against the upturned table. Now in a more aggressive manner Moseley grabbed him by his throat and delivered a third punch which smacked against his jaw. Sullivan fell to the floor, face first. Moseley knew he had rendered him defenceless. He was aware that he needed to keep the sounds low just in case the neighbours had heard the initial confrontation. He found the remote control to the TV and adjusted the level of volume so the roar of the crowd and commentator were increased, but not loud enough to cause offence to the neighbours. He was done with violence for the time being. He looked around the room and saw a sit up straight-backed wooden chair. He went to it, took hold of it by the top and placed it down in the centre of the room. Then he went to Sullivan, slipped his arms under his armpits and hauled him up. Sullivan was half conscious and half out of it.

Manoeuvring him onto his feet Moseley put him in a headlock that threatened to cut off the oxygen to his brain. He managed to turn him one hundred and eighty degrees and force his backside down onto the chair. There was a rivulet of thin almost colourless blood coming out of one nostril and there was reddening on his face from the punch. His shaven pink head was pale but shining with a layer of oil. The old tattoos on his arms had long before lost their colour and were partly hidden by the wrinkles of the skin and by the thick cover of body hair.

Just then the volume coming out of the television increased as the commentator became excited by something happening on the pitch. Sullivan was taking in long breaths of air as if the beating he had taken had expelled the air out of his lungs. With Sullivan in the seat, Moseley grabbed hold of the ball-bearing curtain and yanked it off the door frame. Taking it, he went to the chair and proceeded to wrap the long metal strings around Sullivan and the back of the chair. He worked quickly and soon had him secure with his arms tied tight. Once he was satisfied, Sullivan wouldn't be moving any time soon he turned away and stepped through a door and into a tiny kitchen. He opened a head high cupboard and found what he was looking for – a container of some description – which happened to be a copper pan. He placed the pan under the cold water tap and filled it until it was three-quarters full. Taking the pan handle he stepped back into the room and emptied half of the contents over Sullivan's head. The effect of the cold water, hitting him, quickly had the desired effect. He came alive and gasped out loud. The water drenched his vest. A combination of mucus and blood coming from his nose dripped down his chin.

Moseley then tipped the remaining water over him. Sullivan tried to shake himself free, but the metal strips were tightly wrapped around the back of the chair and his arms so he couldn't get any leverage to prise them off.

Moseley stood over him. "Okay. You fuck. You left me there to die. Didn't you?" He smacked Sullivan across his cheek with an open palm slap. The force was enough to jolt his head and the sound of the blow made a dull thud.

On the TV, advertisements were now playing over a merry jingle. Out through the dust-covered window the spread of the multi-coloured rainbow seats in the football stadium were now in shade. Moseley was trembling, not with fear, but with a desire to hurt Sullivan all he could, but without making him scream. "You left me to die. Didn't you?" he repeated.

Sullivan raised his head and stared at him through his dark eyes. "You don't understand," he said in a tone of voice that contained an acknowledgement of wrong doing.

"Understand what? All I know is that someone drugged me and you let it happen," said Moseley.

"No. Not me."

"I woke up in a fucking dungeon, strapped to a chair with a bright white light blinding me. Like a fucking spy in an interrogation cell. Then some cunt injected me with a chemical and left me to die. And what were you doing all the time this was going on?" He nipped his fingers into his jacket breast pocket, took the end of the syringe, extracted it and put the needle close to Sullivan's eyes. "I swear to God. If I don't get answers. I'll inject you with this deadly shit in here." Sullivan's eyes focused on the combination of milky white liquid and the red of blood inside the tube. Moseley placed the tip of the needle against the flesh on the right-hand side of his neck and gently inserted the tip into his skin. Sullivan tried to free himself. His efforts to snap the chains intensified so he had the chair rocking. Moseley grasped him by the shoulders and pressed down to stop him. He soon gave up the fight.

"What's it going to be? It's down to you."

"Okay. Okay. I'll tell you everything," Sullivan said.

"Talk."

"What do you want to know?"

"What's your connection with Ho Fung?"

"We knew each other when he was in Hong Kong."

"In what sense did you know each other? Were you drinking buddies or summat? Or were you his snitch?" The word 'snitch' was a very emotive word to use. Accusing a police detective of being a snitch was code for a bent copper who fed information to someone who paid for it.

"I was his protector," he revealed.

"Okay. I'm impressed. From what? From who?" Moseley asked.

"I worked for his operation. He used the information I gave him to spy on and get information about some British officials and other high-ranking people in the HK administration at the time.

Moseley had no idea of the structure of the local government or the legislative arm of the authorities in the old British run Hong Kong so couldn't hazard a guess at how high it went. "What else?" he asked.

"Keeping tabs on political enemies," Sullivan said.

"What political enemies?"

"Those working for the pro-democracy movement."

"Where?"

"Here in Hong Kong."

"Explain," said Moseley.

"The Beijing government used him to disrupt the pro-democracy movement before the handover in ninety-seven," Sullivan said.

"Surely Ho Fung was pro-democracy, which is why he got out and went to live in London."

"The reverse," said Sullivan.

"So, what's he doing in London?" Moseley asked.

"I guess he's working for the Beijing government."

"Doing what?"

"Spying on Chinese dissidents. Spying on the British. The Yanks. Who knows? Anyone who could do harm to the Chinese communist party. He's using his influence to lobby on behalf of the Chinese community but spying on them at the same time."

On the television, the second half of the football game was just getting underway. A goal was scored in the first few seconds of the game resuming. The commentator raised his tone of delivery to an increased level of excitement.

"Tell me this," said Moseley. "Did you tell Ho Fung to contact me?"

"Yes."

"Why?"

"He wanted someone who would accept the job without asking too many questions."

"You suggested me?"

"Of course."

"So, I accepted the job. Where does Leo Sinnott come into it? Did Fung pay him to seduce Lily Fung to get her back here from London?"

"Yes."

"Why?" Moseley asked.

"It's simple."

"Is it?"

"Yes."

"What's simple?"

"She was supporting Chinese pro-democracy groups in London."

"What kind of support?"

"Financial mainly. She was using his son's money for Christ's sake. Her brother Lee Wang is a leading figure in the pro-democracy movement here," Sullivan said.

"So, she's giving them money against her father-in-law's wishes. Did her husband know?" Moseley asked.

"Probably not, but I'm not sure. Going against Ho Fung is a big no-no. That's a major issue."

"What happened when he found out?" Moseley asked.

"I guess he told her to stop. I guess she refused."

"Go on," Moseley encouraged.

"So, they planned to entice her back here using Leo Sinnott as a love interest. In a honey trap," said Sullivan.

"It worked."

"Yeah."

Sullivan took in a deep breath through his mouth. The blood in his nostrils had become a thin rivulet. His right eye was puffy where Moseley had punched him. His vest was drenched with a combination of water and blood that had turned the white material a pink and crimson shade.

"What happened when she got back here with Sinnott?" Moseley asked.

"She went to his place and stayed with him," Sullivan replied.

"Then what?"

"She was snatched by a gang."

"Then?"

"Then…? They killed her," said Sullivan.

"Why?"

"To send out a message."

"To who?" Moseley asked.

"To the pro-democracy hot heads."

"Why?"

"To show them that the Hong Kong government has the power to eliminate any threat to the natural order of things."

"Did they need to go to those lengths?"

"I don't know, but I guess they did."

"Stop guessing for fuck sake." Moseley warned.

"They wanted her dead to send a message to not only the Hong Kong dissidents, but those inside Britain as well."

"Geez. This is heavy stuff."

"It's politics. Hong Kong politics. Chinese politics," Sullivan said.

"But why use me?" Moseley asked.

"I guess they wanted to put you in the frame."

"Why me?"

"If she was found dead with a Brit, it might cause a diplomatic incident and discredit the British government, who are poking their nose into Chinese affairs. That's the trouble with the Brits, they never know when to leave things alone."

"But I've got nothing to do with the British government."

"You and I know that. But the implication would be that you're a British agent," said Sullivan.

Moseley was flummoxed by what Sullivan was telling him, but assumed he was telling the truth. "How come you know so much about this?" he asked.

Sullivan didn't reply for a few moments as if he was choosing his words carefully. "I still work for Ho Fung," he confessed.

"You must know him well?"

"He pays for this place and gives me a monthly salary." Sullivan admitted. He looked at Moseley, then at the ball bearing chains wrapped around him. "Are you going to free me from this?" he asked.

"No. I can't say that I am."

"Why? I've told you what I know. That's the deal," he protested.

"No deal."

"Why?" Sullivan asked.

"Because you left me to die in that place." Moseley said.

He put the business end of the needle tight against the flesh of his neck.

“No please,” shouted Sullivan. His cry for mercy was partly lost above the sound coming from the television.

“I hope you enjoy the trip,” said Moseley. He put his finger on the applicator and dug the needle deep into his neck, then pushed down to deliver the content of the tube into his blood. Reaching down he took hold of the metal pan, brought it level, and whacked him in the face with the heavy base. The blow shattered his chin and teeth. His head was jolted back. The blow propelled Sullivan into the middle of next week.

Before he left the flat, Moseley decided to do a search to see if he could find anything of interest. He opened the top drawer of a bureau and rummaged inside. Hidden under some papers there was a thick wad of US one hundred-dollar bills, British pounds, Japanese Yen, and a thick stack of five hundred-dollar Hong Kong notes. He stuffed most of the wads of cash into his trouser and jacket pockets. Then he stepped to the front door, opened it and peered out onto the landing. There was no one about. Before he stepped out, he looked back to see Sullivan. He wasn’t moving. His head was bent back. Sullivan was either out cold or dead. Moseley had little feeling in his heart. He was oblivious to the possibility he may have killed Sullivan. In truth, he didn’t care that much.

He closed the door on the latch then set off along the corridor. Rather than take the lift he opted to walk down the fifteen flights of stairs to the ground floor.

As he stepped off the last step and down into the foyer, he looked at his watch. The time was fast approaching three o'clock. Where had the time gone? He asked himself. He knew there was a British Airways flight leaving Chek Lap Kok airport bound for London at nine-forty that evening. He intended to be on the flight come what may.

Once on the street he walked for several hundred yards towards a busy junction where he came across a line of stationary red taxis at a rank. He got into the first cab and asked the driver to take him to the nearest Metro station from where he could take a subway train across the harbour to the main island.

The taxi driver dropped him close to Jordan metro station.

When the metro train arrived at Wanchai station the time was getting on for four o'clock. He had three hours to get to his hotel, go into his room, pack his things then go to the airport. If he couldn't get on the nine-forty flight, there was another London bound flight leaving at five to midnight.

Once in Wanchai he didn't dawdle. He made it into the front lobby of the hotel. He felt somewhat conspicuous. He still had a pass card so that didn't present a problem to get into his room. He took the lift to the fortieth floor. Once inside the room he had a very quick wash, shaved off the two days of growth on his chin, then changed into a fresh set of clothes. He didn't intend to hang about. There could be people looking for him so it was wise to get out of there as soon as possible. He swiftly emptied the safe then packed his suitcase. He was in two minds about taking the content of the mini-bar, but decided against it.

As soon as he was ready, he left the room and closed the door for the final time. Rather than take the lift he decided to take the emergency exit stairs. It took him ten minutes to walk down the forty flights.

As he finally reached the ground floor, he opened a door that opened onto the lobby. There was a large number of people milling around the desks and sitting in the seats close to the concessionary drinks and snack bar. After a few moments he opened the door, aimed for the wall of light at the glass entrance and stepped around the people, through the hub-hub of sound and towards the exit. He didn't intend to check out. Still anyone observing him would see his suitcase. He moved from the centre of the floor, made it to the wide glass entrance, out the sliding doors and onto the street. He increased his pace and spirited away into the line of pedestrians ambling by the front of the hotel. Once he was out of the range of the hotel, he crossed a busy road, walked by the entrance to a shopping arcade and on towards the nearest taxi rank were two taxis were standing, waiting for passengers.

He opened the door, of the first cab in line, and slid onto the back seat.

"Where you go?" the driver asked.

"The airport," he replied. He had a plane to catch. The bad news was that in the height of the late afternoon rush hour it could take one hour to get to the airport, the good news was that he still had several hours to make the nine-forty flight. If the plane was full, along with the later London flight he intended to take the next one to any destination in western Europe. Paris or Amsterdam or even Frankfurt would suffice. He just wanted to get out of Hong Kong as swiftly as possible.

As he was being driven through the streets of Hong Kong to the airport, he took time to reflect on everything that had happened to him in the past eighty hours. The sheer madness of it all! He was still hounded by the sight of waking up next to the body of someone who he believed to be Lily Fung. It was a memory that would stay with him for a very long time. The explanation Sullivan had given him still left a lot of unanswered questions. Had Ho Fung really gone to those lengths to dispose of his troublesome daughter-in-law? Perhaps the only way to find out was to ask him.

Once in the airport Moseley went straight to the British Airways desk. It was his lucky day. He purchased the last remaining ticket for the nine forty departure to Heathrow. He had to settle for economy over business, but he wasn't bothered. He got the last ticket. He was pleased to be on a flight heading out of Hong Kong with his life still intact.

Chapter 15

The flight was full of Brits going home after trips to Australia and New Zealand, and some expats returning home on business, along with tourists to the UK from mainland China. There wasn't a spare place to be had. Moseley settled down into an aisle seat. He couldn't do a lot but grin and bear it. It was cramped and noisy so he had to suck it in, but he was very relieved to be on his way home after an eventful four days. The in-flight meal was the best airplane food he had ever eaten. Boy was he hungry and thirsty!

The twelve-hour flight time seemed to drag. He spent most of the time watching movie after movie. Most of them instantly forgettable. He did sleep for some of the time but in small periods.

Eleven hours after setting out, the outline of the east coast of England appeared on the monitor screen imbedded into the back of the seat in front of him. He was as good as back home after what was a nightmare of a trip to the Far-East. But it wasn't over. He knew he had to go back to visit Ho Fung in Belgravia to present him with his report and his invoice.

On touchdown in Heathrow he cleared immigration and customs in less than one hour. Rather than take public transport into the centre of the city, he grabbed a taxi from outside Terminal Five to his flat in an apartment building opposite the British Army barracks on Knightsbridge. It felt good to be back in Blighty and on the familiar streets of London. The temperature in the capital was down a good ten degrees from what it had been on the other side of the planet. He was greeted with an overcast sky and drizzle in the air. Still, these were his streets. The place he called home.

Once back in the familiar surroundings of his flat he took a long, hot shower, then went to bed and slept like a baby for the next fourteen hours. It was good to be in the safety of his home. There were a few messages on his answerphone and a couple of emails he had to deal with, but there was nothing to be alarmed about.

He didn't emerge from his bed until late on Monday morning, nearly exactly one week since he had received the telephone call from Ho Fung. Now he had to plan his next move. He had to return to see Mr Fung to inform him that as far as he was concerned the job was over, but it was highly likely that his daughter-in-law was dead.

He had to consider where he went with this. He couldn't very well go to the authorities to tell them the tale for several reasons. He could have killed Leo Sinnott and Laurie Sullivan and going to the police would be breaching client confidentially. Yes, he was home, back in London, but it didn't mean to say this was over by a long way.

If Sullivan was telling the truth and it was all about quelling the anti-Chinese, pro-democracy group in London it could all turn very nasty for him. He didn't want any of that. On a more ethical scale he had to think about the client. There was an unwritten and unspoken code of practice that private investigators don't reveal the content of discussions with clients or reveal the assignments they are on. The only task he was determined to do was to visit the home of Ho Fung and inform him of his findings and to tell him that in his opinion Lily Fung was likely to be dead. Perhaps he might already know this. Maybe he was just seeking confirmation. Moseley didn't know for certain. He wasn't sure of anything anymore.

What was clear was that Ho Fung had known Laurie Sullivan for many years. When Fung had hit on the plan of using a gigolo called Leo Sinnott to entice his daughter-in-law to Hong Kong, he had sought Sullivan's assistance. Sullivan knew of David Moseley from way back when. He knew Moseley was now a private detective working out of an office on Borthwick Street in Soho. Had Sullivan set up the entire operation? There was a chance he had. He had calculated Moseley would be likely to contact him for assistance. The objective of the whole operation was to get Lily Fung back to Hong Kong to kill her and end the alleged funding of a pro-democracy movement of which her brother Lee Wang was a leading member. From here the scenario went down one of two different routes: One, they wanted him to see with his own eyes that Lily Fung was dead, Or, two: they intended to murder him and put him in a position whereby he would be implicated in her death in order to create a kind of diplomatic incident. When they – the bad guys – discovered he wasn't dead and had in effect escaped they removed her body to another location and hid all the evidence. When he returned to the dilapidated fishing hut with Leo Sinnott they intended to try and kill him there and then.

Chapter 16

Two days passed. It was now midday on Wednesday. Moseley had by-and-large recovered from the jet lag. He had spent the previous evening counting the money he had taken from Sullivan's flat. It amounted to quite a tidy sum. There was £2,000 in US dollars. £3,000 in Japanese Yen. £7,000 in Hong Kong dollars, and £6,000 in pounds' sterling. A total of £18,000. A sum of money he would put through his books as money earned from legitimate case work. From Wednesday afternoon onwards he wondered how long he should wait before visiting the home of Ho Fung to present him with his end of assignment report and invoice.

A further day passed. He had heard nothing. No emails. No post. No messages on his business answerphone. He had received an offer of a job from a company who wanted him to spy on a finance manager who they thought was cooking the books and stealing money from them. There was nothing connected to the Ho Fung job.

To put a closure on it he decided to pay a visit to the Belgravia home of Mr Fung on Saturday to seek a meeting with the man who had given him the task.

Saturday afternoon was cool and a little breezy. The days of April were about to become the first days of May. A shower had just dropped its contents over the centre of London, leaving the central streets with a wet sheen and puddles which were now glistening in the sunlight breaking through the clouds. Saturdays in these parts were usually quiet with many of the residents away for the weekend. Therefore, there was little traffic on the roads.

In Belgravia there wasn't a lot happening. The cars parked tight into the side of Seaton Place told of fine taste and few money concerns. The facades of the homes with their white walls, metal grills, first-floor balconies, and colonnade porches, gave the appearance of a classy, highly sophisticated London neighbourhood. Which it very much was.

Moseley walked along the pavement. He was dressed in a dark suit. He held a document holder wedged under his arm. He hadn't made an appointment, but guessed there was an even chance that Mr Fung would be at home. If he was it would be interesting to see how he greeted him.

He was soon at the front of the four-storey house with the step up to the front door and the steps down to the basement. A quick glance over the ground floor rails and down the concrete steps revealed a door at the bottom of the stairs.

He moved onto the raised step and took the several short paces to the front door with its stout, gold-plate decorative knocker, gold plate letterbox and door button in the intercom unit under the shade of the overhead balcony. He pressed the door button.

Thirty seconds passed with no one answering his call, so he hit the button again. Then he heard a voice coming out of the intercom enquiring: "Who is it?" Asked by someone with an oriental sounding accent.

"It's David Moseley, of Moseley Private Investigations, here to see Mr Fung," he replied.

Silence. One minute passed. Moseley was beginning to think the door would remain closed to him, when he heard the sound of the lock opening. The solid slab of polished wood moved inward to a narrow degree and the eyes of a male with Chinese features appeared in the opening.

"Yes. I help you?" he asked in faltering English.

"It's Mr Moseley to see Mr Fung," he replied.

"What your business?"

"I've got a report for Mr Fung," said Moseley and held the document holder in front of his midriff.

The door opened slightly wider. The fellow on the other side looked to be in his mid-thirties. He was wearing a pinstriped jacket, matching waistcoat and trousers combination, a white shirt and a dark tie which had a large knot tucked into the neck. He looked at the document holder then at Moseley and gave him an up and down inspection.

"Mr Fung. He is expecting you? Yes," he asked.

"No," replied Moseley. "He's not expecting me."

"So, what your business?"

"I have the report Mr Fung requested," Moseley replied.

The chap looked at him with a combination of uncertainty and confusion forming a squint in his eyes and a pout along his lips. "He knows you coming?" he asked.

"No. As I said, I want to give him a report."

"What report?"

"My final report and invoice on the search for Lily Fung."

The chap didn't reply for a long moment and continued to look at Moseley with a pinched-eye expression of puzzlement and uncertainty. "One moment," he said and promptly closed the door on him.

Moseley waited. A minute passed. He turned towards the path and took a couple of steps back and moved out from under the shade of the balcony. As he stepped back, the door opened and an imposing looking guy with a wide girth, thick chest and a Charlie Chan type of moustache appeared in the doorway and stood in the frame in a wide-legged stance. The guy in the pinstriped jacket, waistcoat and trouser combo was standing at his side.

"Come in," said the larger man and took a sideways step.

Moseley nodded his head to him, then took a few steps and entered through the door and into the white marble vestibule room with its authentic Hong Kong British flag in the glass case attached to the wall and the gleaming gold leaf dragon statues. There was a smell of burning incense sticks in the air.

The bigger guy, was at least six feet tall and he must have weighed twenty stone. He looked at Moseley. "I search you?" he asked.

"Sure."

Moseley put the document holder down and rested it in between his ankles, then he raised his arms and held them level with his shoulders. He had expected to be greeted by the housemaid. Not two men. This was a surprise. The chap patted him down in a professional manner which seemed to suggest he had done this on many occasions before. Then his eyes went to the document holder and he gestured to it. Moseley took the holder and passed it into his hand. He opened the zip and looked inside for any concealed weapons or anything of a suspicious nature. When he was satisfied it was clean, he gave it back to him.

Just then Moseley was aware of a man in his seventies gingerly coming down the staircase in a slow careful ascent. He was wearing a cashmere mustard coloured cardigan over a plain, button-down shirt, and grey flannel trousers.

He stepped off the last stair and came to join the three men assembled close to the front door. The other two stepped to a side to let him take the central position. Moseley had never seen him before in his life, but he looked strikingly similar to the man in the grainy photograph of Ho Fung, he had viewed online, and remarkedly similar to the man he had met previously.

"Yes. Who are you?" he asked directly to Moseley.

"I'm here to give Mr Fung my report," Moseley said.

The chap had heavy-lidded brown eyes, and a slim, slightly pugged nose. His teeth were the same colour as his olive skin.

"I am Mr Fung," he said stiffly and looked at Moseley through inquisitive eyes.

He wasn't the Mr Fung; Moseley had spoken to twelve days before. He looked at him and smiled.

"No, Mr Ho Fung."

"But I am Mr Ho Fung," he repeated bluntly and glanced at the two men at his side.

"I was here on Monday. Not the Monday just gone," said Moseley losing his train of thought for a moment … "the week before. I spoke to a man who said he was Ho Fung."

"I wasn't here, last week," said the elderly chap. The other two men didn't say a word. Both had edged closer to the older man. Not for the first time in the last few days Moseley wondered if he had dreamt all this, or if it was part of a new dream? Or something far sinister.

"But the man asked me to go to Hong Kong to find his daughter-in-law, Lily Fung. Locate her and bring her back to London. Here look at this…." he unzipped the document holder, reached inside and withdrew the photograph Ho Fung had given him.

He offered it to the man who seemed reluctant to take it, but he relented. He took the photograph from him and looked at the figures for a few fleetingly moments. His eyes gave nothing away. He handed the photograph back to Moseley.

"I know no-one in this," he replied stiffly.

The guy in the pinstriped jacket said something in a language Moseley couldn't understand. The older man replied in short shrift. "What's this about?" he asked Moseley.

Moseley narrowed his eyes. "I received a telephone call from a man who called himself Ho Fung a week last Monday. He asked me to come to this house…" He looked around to take in the wood panelled door leading into the reception room where the meeting had taken place. "We talked in there," he thrust his chin in the direction of the room, just a few feet away… "about his daughter-in-law called Lily Fung and that he wanted me to go to Hong Kong to find her then bring her back to London."

"Lily is at home in Kensington with her husband. My son Hue," the chap replied.

"So, who did I find *dead* on the bed?" Moseley asked.

The mention of the word *'dead'*, caused the other two men to look at each other. Something was very amiss here. If the man he had spoken to previously wasn't Ho Fung then who the hell was he? Moseley was plunged into a deep chasm of uncertainty. Not for the first time he had to ask himself what in God's name was going on.

He looked at the tip of his shoes then raised his head and looked into the eyes of the man who had said he was Ho Fung.

"Do you know an ex-police officer in the Hong Kong police called Laurie Sullivan?" he asked.

The man considered the question for the briefest of moments, then he shook his head, but didn't say a word.

"Do you know a racehorse trainer called Leo Sinnott?" asked Moseley. He observed his eyes to see if his pupils diluted to reveal he did know the name or they closed to reveal the opposite. The man shook his head for a second time. His pupils remained pretty much the same size. Something completely and utterly off the wall was going on. Moseley considered for the first time that the man in front of him was an imposter, or that the man in front of him was the real

Ho Fung and that someone else had given him the brief to go to Hong Kong to find someone who was apparently alive and well and living in Kensington. If that was the case, what the hell was going on?

Was one of the men at his side responsible for the set-up? If so, what was his goal? Or was the man in front of him, the one who said he was Ho Fung, somebody else. If so, what was his objective? The two men who said they were Ho Fung did have similarities. They were the same age. The same stature and physical dimensions. They had the same, thick spikey grey hair. The same facial features. One of them was the real Ho Fung. The other was an imposter. But who was the real one? Moseley had no idea. According to Sullivan, he and Fung knew each other well, consequently this guy must have been lying. He also knew Leo Sinnott because he trained his racehorses. He had lied again. Moseley looked at the three men, then sought to wriggle out of this.

"Sorry, I must be mistaken," he said. "I'm so sorry to have bothered you with this. I have the wrong Mr Fung. Please accept my sincere apology."

None of the three men replied. They watched as Moseley took a step back and edged to the door whilst keeping his eyes on the three of them. He turned, one-eighty, opened the front door and moved out under the overhanging porch. The man, in the pinstriped suit, who had opened the door stepped forward, followed him to the end of the porch then paused and watched him walk away along the path. Moseley carried on, walked by the wrought iron fence and the gate leading onto the stairs that led down to the basement, then away from the house.

He wondered what his next move should be. Should he forget about the whole thing or should he continue the investigation? More than one person was deceased, therefore maybe he should continue to try and discover what it was all about. He simply couldn't forget about it. With this thought going through his head he pondered on how he could gain access to the house. The short flight of eight steps going down to the basement could be a way to get inside.

He soon made it to the street off Sloane Square where he had parked his car on a meter. He was back in Seaton Place within twenty-five minutes of leaving the house. The time was edging close to three o'clock. He managed to find a parking space about one hundred yards from the front of the house. He knew he couldn't stay here for too long. The parking wardens in this neck of Chelsea and Kensington were known to be keen. They would slap a ticket on a non-resident's vehicle in the blink of an eye. He knew that he had to find another way of obtaining answers. It was at this point he considered asking for assistance from a chap called Bob Ambrose.

Ambrose owed him a favour from six months before, when Moseley had done some surveillance work for him. It was now time for Ambrose to pay his debt.

He had known Ambrose for several years. Ambrose worked for himself as a designer and installer of high-tech surveillance systems, security detectors and eavesdropping equipment. He was in a similar line of work to Moseley. He had been in the Met police at the same time as Moseley, therefore they knew each other well. Ambrose just happened to be a good break-in-and-enter exponent. They hadn't spoken to each other for about a year. Moseley had him on speed dial on his phone. He called him from his car. Ambrose picked it up on the fifth ring.

"Bob Ambrose Security systems," he said.

"It's Dave Moseley. Long-time no see. I need a favour doing."

Ambrose had a reputation for being laconic, serious and deadpan. "Such has?" he enquired.

"A B and E on a house in Belgravia."

"Reason."

"A job."

"Fire away."

"You won't believe me if I told you."

"Try me."

Moseley told Ambrose the full story of how he had gone to Hong Kong to try and find the daughter-in-law of a rich Chinese man and everything that had occurred to him. It was true, Ambrose didn't believe him. He was finding it hard to believe what sounded like the scenario of some far-fetched movie. Moseley tended to agree with him.

"What do you want me to do?" Ambrose asked.

"Help me break into the house to see who and what I can discover," Moseley replied.

"When and what time?" Ambrose asked.

"Tomorrow morning at one o'clock."

"Where?" Ambrose asked.

"Seaton Place."

Ambrose said nothing for a long moment. As if he was considering the request. Moseley stayed silent.

"Okay," said Ambrose without further question or debate. He must have known Moseley would call him one day and ask him to repay the debt in time and energy. That day had come.

Chapter 17

At one o'clock on a Sunday morning, Belgravia was quiet. Nothing much stirred along Seaton Place. The low glow of lights in several of the homes were visible behind drawn curtains. The good people of Belgravia were settling down for the night. The streetlights bathed the roadway in a patchy splash of illumination. As there were a few embassies in this part of town, the area was well-policed. This did give Moseley plenty of concern about this operation. If he was going to gain access to the house, then he might have to take a few chances. His car was parked on the street in a spot three hundred yards from the front of the Fung residence.

At the bottom of the street the dark shape of the inlet leading to the tree-lined grassy square was just visible at the end of the cul-de-sac.

Moseley's mobile phone rang. It was Bob Ambrose telling him that he was just about to enter the street. With the area they were in and the relatively early hour of the day, it was a tricky situation to put it mildly. It would have been better if it was a weekday and perhaps later in the morning, but this is what it was. If they managed to break-in into the house, they just might be able to get in without setting off an alarm. This is where Ambrose's expertise would come in handy. The notice about a neighbourhood watch scheme pinned to several lamp-posts may have been a ruse to put off any potential opportunist burglars. Ambrose said he would come prepared with the tricks of the trade, such as a bunch of skeleton keys, a can of quick expanding foam to knock out any alarm boxes and reflective metal strips to place over any motion sensors.

The most obvious point of entry to the Fung house was down the stairs to the door leading into the basement, rather than through the back garden which was probably secured by a high barb-wire topped fence and security lights that would come on when activated by movement. If they did gain entry via the basement door, they may be able to gain access to the rest of the house, but there was no guarantee of success.

It had just turned five past one when Ambrose pulled up in a space behind Moseley's BMW. He killed the engine and turned the headlights off. Then he got out of his car, opening and closing the door with the least sound possible. He slipped into Moseley's car and sat on the back seat. He was carrying a canvas bag in his hand.

Bob Ambrose was taller than the average bloke. A slim, good looking fifty-year-old. He had been in the Serious Crime squad in the Met police before a purge of the ranks got rid of him and several other guys. He had used his detective skills and contacts to turn in a new direction. He went into the security game. He worked for several companies and organisations as a freelance. He even supplied security expertise for several embassies in the city and organisations, then branched out into the service sector. It was the best thing he ever did, so he said.

His hair, which was plentiful, was now almost grey-white. The moustache and goatee beard combo suited his quirky nature. He was wearing black jeans and a black sweatshirt under a zip-up jacket, also in a shade of black.

"What's the score?" he asked.

Moseley filled him in again. The details hadn't changed since the last time he had spoken to him on the telephone at ten o'clock.

Moseley looked up the street. "The target house is in complete dark. It's the last but one at the end of the row on the left."

Ambrose looked up the street, while Moseley continued to update him. "Lights were on in a first-floor room at the front until about eleven-thirty, then lights in a second and third floor windows came on."

Ambrose looked at his watch. "Let's give them to one-thirty," he requested.

"Okay. I'm in no rush," replied Moseley.

Moseley looked to a side to observe an urban fox, which must have come from the tree-lined area at the bottom of the road, nonchalantly wander along the path. It stopped then looked at their car as if it had detected a sound from inside. Moseley wondered if this was an omen, either good or bad. Ambrose also saw the fox, but didn't comment.

Neither of them said anything for a few minutes, then it was Ambrose who broke the silence. "What do you know about the inside of the house?" he enquired.

"Not a great deal," Moseley replied. "Plenty of rooms as you would expect in a property of that size. Inside on the ground floor is a staircase going up to the first floor."

"Any internal lift?" Ambrose asked.

"Probably," Moseley replied.

"How about the back?"

"Not sure."

"What about an alarm system?"

"I never saw evidence of any. But I wasn't looking for one," Moseley said.

"So, you didn't see any motion detectors? CCTV cameras or anything like that?"

"No. There's not any that I know of."

"There's bound to be something. I've got some bits and pieces in my bag. How about any people?"

"Three men when I came this afternoon."

"Age ranges?" Ambrose asked.

"Two guys in their thirties, another older guy in his seventies."

"Guards?"

"May have been."

"Size?"

"One large. The other no size," Moseley said.

"Okay."

Ambrose looked at his watch again. "Mind if I smoke?"

"Feel free," Moseley said.

Ambrose took a pack of cigarettes from his jacket pocket, took one out and lit it with a lighter. The car was soon full of the aroma of tobacco and mist of blue-grey fumes.

Twenty-five minutes of silence passed. There was no movement on the street. Several of the lights in the houses were now out. Residents were retiring for the night.

It was exactly one-thirty when they got out of the car with the least sound possible. Once out they quickly crossed over to the other side of the road and walked up the pathway at a quick pace. Within a matter of twenty seconds or so they were at the front of the house. The noise of a living city played out its cacophony of background sound. There was no breeze to speak of. The air was still and in no way chilly. There were lights on in some of the homes, but the majority were in dark.

On reaching the Fung residence Ambrose took hold of the metal gate in the wrought iron fence and opened it. Luckily the hinges didn't squeak. He stepped down the eight steep steps to the area in front of the door that led into the basement. Moseley closed the gate behind him, then followed Ambrose down the steps. Under the shade of the front of the house above them, the door was hardly visible. It was a plain door with nine glass panes in the top half and a hardwood panel beneath.

Ambrose tried the handle. It was locked. He tried it again and this time he put extra leverage behind his shoulder. When he forced it, it soon became obvious that it wasn't bolted from the inside. Ambrose put the canvas bag on the floor, opened it and reached inside. The first thing he extracted was a pencil torch, then a bunch of long keys with different shaped serrated edges. He turned the torch on then aimed the beam at the keyhole. The light reflected in the glass panes in the door. He delved into the bag again, felt inside and extracted a thin section of rolled metal six inches long. It had a flat surface at one end. The second item he extracted from the bag was a roll of something that looked like a child's plasticine. He ripped some off in his fingers and placed it onto the flat end surface of the bar, then flattened it with his thumb and forefinger. He threaded the end of the metal into the keyhole. The plasticine would take an imprint of the internal lock.

He withdrew the implement from the lock and put the torch light onto the plasticine to see the imprint the lock made. Then he quickly looked through the bunch of keys until he found one that just about matched the imprint. He then took the key off the ring, inserted it into the lock and flicked his wrist to turn the key. He didn't say a word. He reached into his inside jacket pocket and took out a slim, sharp pointed piece of metal that resembled a nail file. He fitted this into the lock, with the key still inside. Using both hands he wriggled the tools. In the next instant, the door bolt snapped open.

Before doing another thing, he put the tools into the bag, then took hold of the door handle and turned it. The door opened to reveal the pitch-black inside. He took the torch and aimed the beam in and ran it along the door frame.

"Seems okay," he whispered.

"What's okay?" Moseley asked.

"Doesn't appear that there are any wires or detectors in here. We could be in. Follow me. Do as I do."

Ambrose got down onto his hands and knees then shuffled forward and over the raised threshold running across the opening. Moseley got down on his knees, then on to his stomach and followed Ambrose as he crawled on all fours into a corridor and into the pitch-black inside of the basement. Underneath them was a bare concrete floor. The air tasted cold and fusty as if the basement hadn't been used for some time.

Ambrose lifted the torch and spread the beam along the length of a corridor. There were a set of five steps at the bottom end that led up to an internal door. Ambrose concentrated the beam on the surrounds of the door, looking for some form of detection device. He couldn't see one so he got to his feet. Moseley did likewise. There were two closed doors along the length of the corridor that led into rooms on each side. Ambrose put the light on the flights of stairs then onto the lock in the door.

"This must lead to the ground floor," he said.

Moseley had already guessed that. Ambrose took the lead. He picked up the tool bag, took a few steps to the bottom of the steps, then up them to the second door. He gave Moseley the torch and asked him to put the beam on the lock. Ambrose got hold of the door handle and forced it down. The door was locked. He delved into bag again and withdrew the skeleton keys and the secondary device. He repeated the same procedure, found the required key and threaded it into the lock. He gave it a twist. The door partly opened so he took the nail file and slid the hooked end into the keyhole and manipulated it. The bolt opened. He took the handle, turned it and the door popped open.

It opened onto a dimly-lit area with the smooth marble surface. Ambrose asked Moseley for the torch, took it from him, and immediately wafted the light along the corridor. He took the final step and moved off the last step, through the door and onto the ground floor. Moseley was a few feet behind him. The light, from a fixed wall lamp on a dimmer switch, left a reflection on the floor. A few feet to one side was a single silver-metal door. Moseley had guessed right. The house did have a lift. The call button was embedded in a silver aluminium plate.

Moseley moved past Ambrose, stepped by the lift door then came to the end of the corridor and into the vestibule. So far, so good. They were in the house and hadn't come across any detection devices. The front door was just across the shiny marble surface. The window at the side looked out onto the street. The gold-leaf cover on the dragon statues caught the streetlight. A corridor led to a second door that must have led into the back of the house.

Moseley turned to look at Ambrose. "There's the stairs," he whispered.

"Which way?" asked Ambrose.

Moseley glanced to the door that must have led into the back section of the ground floor. "Let's see where this goes." He pointed at the door.

He took the lead, grasped hold of the handle and opened the door. It led into a large glass roof conservatory which was full of large glass plant pots, containing an assortment of huge flowers and shrubs. The smell was like a garden. The light of the moon was raining through the glass roof so everything was bathed in light and shade. A pair of French windows led out onto the garden that was bathed in moonlight.

Moseley turned back. "Let's go back and up to the first floor," he suggested.

They crept back along the corridor and into the area by the front door and the carpeted staircase. Moseley looked up the stairs to see a lamp light on the landing and an antique painting attached to the wall at the summit.

This was now becoming scary. If the two men he had met this afternoon appeared, there was bound to be a kerfuffle. Hopefully, there were no more than two of them.

Moseley moved onto the first step and ascended the stairs; Ambrose was a few steps behind him. At the top of the stairs, Moseley turned onto the first-floor landing. There was a corridor leading into the back of the house and doors to rooms along the length. There was no sound. The deep pile of the carpet beneath their feet effectively cushioned the sound of their movement. A clock, with a gold plate face, high on the wall, was a few minutes fast.

Moseley made it along the landing to the door that led into a room at the front of the house. The one that opened onto the first-floor balcony. He opened it gently and poked his head around the frame. A lamp light was on low. It was a lounge room that went across the width of the front. There was a large sofa in the centre and an assortment of furniture. Art on the walls and various other artefacts like expensive looking pots and vases dotted here and there. Some of them no doubt genuine Ming-dynasty. Floor to ceiling shiny gold fabric curtains were closed over the high windows.

Moseley backed out and closed the door behind him, again with the least sound possible. He pointed up to the next floor. Ambrose nodded his head.

Moseley took the first step up to the second floor. He was conscious there were two more floors. The house was huge, twenty plus rooms without a doubt. They made it up the stairs onto the second floor, then along the landing to the door of the room above the lounge on the first floor. This must have been a bedroom.

Moseley tried it, but it was locked. Bob Ambrose, had it open in less than half a minute. Moseley carefully opened the door. Inside, a low pink light was shining from a lamp to illuminate the room in a kind of subdued half-light. It illuminated the figure of a woman who was laid flat on a mattress. She was dressed in night attire, but the most striking thing was that her wrists and ankles were tied by a restraint. Moseley didn't recognise her immediately. It took him several long moments to see it was the housemaid who had shown him into the house when he visited on the first occasion.

It was as strange as it was bizarre. What had she done that had resulted in someone wanting to tie her up? Moseley looked at Ambrose and they shared a face. There was clearly some skulduggery going on in here. Moseley couldn't smell anything. There was no whiff of alcohol or drugs. The room was just like an average, everyday standard bedroom: a bed, a storage unit, an in-built wardrobe unit on one side and several chests of drawers, plus a fancy armoire. Lacy curtains were drawn closed over the window.

The figure on the bed suddenly moved and let out a snore. In the next instant, she opened her eyes and saw the strangers in the room. Moseley immediately put a finger to his lips.

"Shhhh," he said. Ambrose stepped into the room and closed the door behind him. Just then there was a sound of feet on the stairs coming down from the third floor.

A few moments passed then the door opened and the smaller of the two men, Moseley had met earlier that day, entered the room. He clapped his eyes on the two intruders and immediately sought to get out. He was wearing a plain white singlet and boxer type dark underwear. Before he could shout out or move, Moseley grabbed him around the head and clamped his hand over his mouth. He fought with him for a few moments to get control. It was only then that Moseley saw the black object in the grip of his right hand. He whacked him on the wrist with his fist which caused him to drop a firearm to the floor. Ambrose swiftly retrieved the gun, then clubbed the chap with a punch that buckled his legs. Moseley let go of him and the chap fell to the floor like a tree felled by a single strike of an axe. He was out stone cold.

Moseley didn't know if the lady spoke English. "Where is Ho Fung?" he asked slowly. The sight of the gun had spooked him.

She looked up at the ceiling. "On the next floor," she replied, her words were heavily distorted by an accent.

"Is he okay?" She didn't reply immediately. She looked stunned that there were two strangers in the room who had come to help her. "Where is Ho Fung?" Moseley asked again. "Is he okay?"

"He's been held prisoner. Like me," she said quickly.

Moseley set about the task of untying her and soon had her wrists and ankles free of the restraints. He took her by the arms and pulled her upright, then put her down so she was sitting on the edge of the mattress. He put a pillow behind her back to help to prop her up. She rubbed her wrists. Moseley threw the restraints, two pieces of platted, twisted cord to Ambrose.

"Use these to tie him up," he advised.

Ambrose took the cord and did as he was requested. He put the semi-conscious man onto his front, pulled his arms back, tied his wrists together and extended it to tie his ankles with the same length of cord.

Moseley looked at the lady. She looked none the worse for the ordeal she was going through. "How many of them are there?" he asked.

She hesitated for a moment as if she didn't understand the question. "Three," she responded after a few seconds.

"Is Ho Fung being guarded?" he asked.

She looked confused, before she understood the question. "Yes," she replied.

"We'll be back in a moment," said Moseley. He looked to Ambrose. "Fung's upstairs. The other one is guarding him."

He turned back to the lady. “Is someone pretending to be Ho Fung?” he asked her.

Again, she was a little slow understanding the question. Then she nodded her head. “Yes. Yes. That is right,” she replied.

“Okay. We’ll try to free him,” said Moseley. He looked to Ambrose who was examining the handgun. “Let’s go and get the other two.”

Ambrose suddenly looked put out by what was happening. “Eh. I didn’t sign up for this,” he uttered. It was getting too heavy for him.

“Neither did I, but we’re here now,” said Moseley. “Ho Fung is super rich. You’ll be well rewarded. I can guarantee that,” he added.

The suggestion of impending financial reward seemed to end Ambrose’s desire to back out. He didn’t say a word. He followed Moseley out of the room. Just as they were stepping onto the landing the thick-set guy with the Charlie Chan set of whiskers was coming down the stairs at a pace. He seemed keen to tackle Moseley, but when he saw there were two of them, he hesitated.

Ambrose raised the semi-automatic handgun and levelled it at him. “Down you come,” he ordered.

The man turned and set off to run back up the stairs, but he was a large, ungainly fellow. He didn’t have the turn of pace. Moseley reached out, grabbed his ankles, yanked his legs back and brought him down to the ground. He fell face first onto the edge of the stairs. Moseley took his feet and pulled him down the final six stairs. His chin banged against the edge of each stair. As he turned his head Moseley punched him in the face. He screamed out loud once before Moseley was able to clap his hand over his mouth. The guy tried to bite him. Moseley managed to pull his hand away from his mouth. "Find something to tie him with," Moseley said to Ambrose while he continued to hold the fellow down.

Ambrose went into bedroom. He came out twenty seconds later with a sash cord from a curtain. He handed it to Moseley who used it to tie the man's hands behind his back. Once the man was well and truly secure, they hoisted him up and manoeuvred him into the second-floor bedroom and put him down alongside the other one.

Then Moseley and Ambrose went out of the room and took the stairs to the third floor. On the landing, Moseley approached the front room at the bottom of the corridor. If the lady was correct, Ho Fung was in this room.

Moseley looked to Ambrose. "Cover me," he said. He waited for a moment. When he felt his adrenalin peak, he flew at the door, took the handle and pushed on it. The door was locked. This time Moseley didn't wait for Ambrose to open it with his tools. He lifted his foot, aimed it against the door and kicked against the panel. The bolt snapped, and the door flew open.

Moseley pushed the door open and stepped inside. The room was illuminated by the light from a single lamp. The man who Moseley knew to be Ho Fung was lying on a king-size bed. His head resting on a pillar. Then Moseley could see Fung's hands were tied in front of him. Moseley went to him. He was wearing a towel like robe over a vest and plain pyjama bottoms.

In order not to frighten him, Moseley took him gently by the shoulders and gave him a light shake. “Mr Fung. Mr Fung. Can you hear me?” he asked. Fung opened his eyes and looked up to see Moseley leaning over him. “It’s me, David Moseley,” he said. “Are you okay?” he asked.

“I know you,” Fung said in a hesitant, confused manner. “You’re the man who came to the house.”

“That’s right. Who tied you up?” Moseley asked.

“What?”

“Who tied you?” Moseley repeated.

“They did.”

“Why?”

“Why!” He hesitated. “Because they want you to believe that he is the real me.”

“Who?”

“The man you saw today.”

“You know I was here today, trying to see you?” Moseley asked.

“He tell me.”

“Who told you?”

“The man who is pretending to be me.”

“Who is he?” Moseley asked.

“A man called Wan Jok.”

“What is he to you?”

"He was my assistant," replied Fung.

"I thought that was the case," said Moseley. He untied Fung's hands, then helped him to sit on the edge of the mattress and to get him to his feet. After a few moments to get over the shock and sudden movement, Moseley led Fung out of the room, along the landing and down the stairs to the second-floor.

In the second-floor bedroom the lady was still sitting on the edge of the mattress. Both the kidnappers were lying tied-up on the floor.

Ambrose followed Fung into the room. He looked at Moseley. "What you gonna do?" he asked.

"Get them out of here."

"I thought you said there were three of them."

"The other guy must be elsewhere."

Moseley escorted the lady and Mr Fung all the way down the stairs to the ground floor. Moseley had freed both Mr Fung and the housemaid. Perhaps the smart thing to do would be to get them out of the house and call the police for assistance and to report a case of unlawful abduction and kidnap.

"I'll take them out through the basement, then I'll call the police," Moseley said to Ambrose.

"I don't want anything to do with the *police*," said Ambrose concerned that the word *police* had been used.

"That's okay. I won't mention your involvement or your name," said Moseley.

"Okay. But there's one thing."

"What?"

"Remember it was me who helped. Won't you?" he said looking at Mr Fung and thinking about his riches.

"Of course, I will," said Moseley.

Ambrose led the way along the corridor, around the corner, then through the open door leading into the basement, down the steps, along the corridor, then out and into the cool of the early morning.

The four of them, Moseley, Mr Fung, the housemaid, and Ambrose walked up the steps, out of the gate, along the pavement and away from the house.

Moseley went to his car, opened the back door, and shepherded both Fung and the lady onto the back seat. He closed the door, then he climbed into the driver's seat, took his smart phone, and tapped 9-9-9 into the number pad. Meanwhile, Ambrose got into his car, started the engine, pulled away from the kerb and drove away up the street and disappeared around the corner. He didn't want anything to do with the police and who could blame him? This incident still had legs and it wasn't over by a long way.

Chapter 18

The 9-9-9 call was answered within five rings. Moseley asked for the police. He was transferred to the Metropolitan Police desk. A female operator asked him what was the nature of his call.

"I want to report a break-in at number eighty-six Seaton Place in Belgravia," he said.

"What's your name?" she asked.

"David Moseley."

"Where are you calling from?"

"Right outside the house on the street."

"How do you know there's been a break in?" she asked.

"I broke in," he replied.

The operator suspected it was a crank call. "Why would you break in?"

"Because I had to find if Mr Fung was alive and well."

"Who is Mr Fung?"

"My client."

"How did you break in?"

"Through a door and into the basement."

"The basement?"

"That's right." Moseley suspected that the operator was trying to keep him talking to put a trace on the call.

"What did you find in the house?"

"The housemaid and Mr Fung have been abducted by three men, tied up and held against their will."

"By whom?"

"The other men," he replied.

"Where are they?" she asked.

"Who?"

"The three men!" she said with the hint of a question mark in her tone.

"In the house. I tackled two of them."

"By yourself?"

"With help."

"From whom?" she asked.

"A friend…Look are the police on their way?"

"Where is the other one?"

"What other one?"

"You said there are three men."

"He's still inside the house someplace or somewhere else."

"Where are you calling from?"

"My car."

"Wait there."

"Are the police on their way?" Moseley asked.

"I've despatched a car to the address."

"Thanks," said Moseley then hung up before she could utter another word.

He turned to face Mr Fung and the lady who were both sitting close together for comfort and warmth. They had just escaped from a traumatic experience. After all, being trussed up and held captive in your own home couldn't have been much fun. He didn't want to carry out an interview in his car, but had no other option.

He looked at Mr Fung. The streetlight was slanting across his face to highlight the lines and the wrinkles by his eyes. His skin had a pale-yellow tint and the pigment marks were like brown gravy spots. His hair was sticking up and unkempt. He didn't look as polished as he had done the other day. In the robe, over the pyjamas, he had the appearance of a rich, eccentric aristocrat who walked around all day in his nightwear and couldn't be bothered to dress himself.

"I've got some bad news for you," Moseley announced.

"Did you find her?" Fung asked, perhaps guessing that he was referring to Lily Fung.

"I found your daughter-in-law. I'm sorry to say it's not good news."

"Is she…" he didn't want to utter the dreaded word that was on the tip of his tongue. He could guess by the mournful expression on Moseley's face that she was dead. He held out a thick curved hand to the lady, she took it and tenderly cradled his fingers.

"Will you level with me?" Moseley asked. Fung didn't reply. "Did you pay Leo Sinnott to romance her and whisk her to Hong Kong?"

"No. Her brother did that," he replied softly.

"Why would he do that?" Moseley asked.

"The government in Hong Kong knew she was using the family wealth to fund a pro-independence movement. They had a spy in their number. Lee Wang."

"Her brother?" Moseley asked for clarification.

"That is right" Fung said. "He pay Leo Sinnott to come here to take her to Hong Kong so that they could threaten her to stop her funding the group. But they kill her."

Moseley tried to make some sense of the confusion and the underlying connections. He was finding it extremely difficult to grasp them. The lady released Fung's hand. He ran the tips of his fingers through his hair.

"How do you know she dead?" Fung asked.

"I was drugged with a shot of something. I woke up a few days later and found myself in a semi-derelict building by a beach on the south side of the island. I was probably not supposed to survive, but I did. Then I saw the dead body next to me. I'm sorry to say it was your daughter-in-law, Lily Fung."

Fung put his flat palms to his face to cover his eyes. Moseley gave him a few seconds to regain some of his composure. "Why would her brother want to set her up?" Moseley asked.

"The Hong Kong government must have promised him big job for helping them. They would make him an important man on the council body. That would make him popular in Beijing."

"Let me get this right," said Moseley, still unconvinced by his explanation. "Her brother contacted Leo and paid him to come to London to begin an affair with her?" Fung didn't respond. "He has to be a pretty lowlife character to do that to his own sister." Moseley thought it didn't stack up. It didn't seem quite right, but maybe, in this crazy scenario it had some semblance of truth.

Moseley turned back to Mr Fung. "Do you know an Englishman by the name of Laurie Sullivan?" he asked.

"Yes."

"What is your connection to him?"

"Laurie Sullivan work for me in Hong Kong. He was a police officer in the Hong Kong force."

"What did he do for you?" Moseley asked.

"He gave me information on criminals' activities."

"He was a paid informer?"

"Yes."

"Why?"

"So, I know what is going on all the time and what those who could hurt my business are doing," Fung replied.

"Who does he work for now?"

"I not know."

"How did you know to contact me?"

"I remember him telling me that you are a private investigator in London. When I wanted someone to try and find Lily, I remember you."

Moseley assumed it was a total coincidence that he had sought Sullivan's assistance. The smart money told him the old man knew of the connection between the two of them and used it as a way of finding his daughter-in-law.

"So, you don't work for the Beijing government as a spy?"

Fung looked genuinely aghast at such a suggestion. "Who say that?" he asked in a piqued tone.

"Laurie Sullivan."

"He lie," said Fung adamantly.

Moseley sighed then turned to face the windscreen and look up the street. He had no idea how he was going to explain all this to the police when they arrived.

In the next second, a saloon car appeared on the street and drove past them at a fast pace.

Chapter 19

Moseley watched the vehicle go up the street towards the backdrop of trees at the end of the cul-de-sac. It came to a halt directly opposite number eighty-six. Moseley looked at his watch. The time was fast approaching two-fifteen.

He turned back to Fung. “I’ll be ten minutes. Fifteen max,” he said. “There’s something I have to do.” He got out of his car, leaving Mr Fung and the housemaid sitting on the back seat. He crossed the road and walked up the pavement to the house. He was aware of another car coming up behind him and turned to see a marked Metropolitan Police vehicle go by. It pulled up close to the unmarked car. Two uniformed police officers got out of the police car, looked up at the front of eighty-six, then approached the unmarked car.

Moseley quickened his pace and was soon at the front of the house. The two uniformed cops observed him. Then the front doors of the unmarked car opened and two guys in civilian clothes got out and joined their uniformed colleagues on the pavement outside the door to number eighty-six.

One of the cops in uniform clocked Moseley. “Who are you?” he called out to him.

“I’m the guy who called you. Dave Moseley,” he replied.

“Moseley,” said one of the plain clothes cops in a raised voice. Moseley immediately knew who he was. He was a former Serious Crime squad member by the name of Peter Randall.

DCI Peter Randall was a long serving cop in that unit. Moseley had known him for a few years, though he hadn't seen him or spoken to him since the day he left the service. He knew that Randall was now a senior officer in the Diplomatic Protection Service. Perhaps he had gone back to the Serious Crime Unit in the recent past.

The streetlight was reflecting on Randall's bald pate. He wore what remained of his hair in a short close to the bone fashion. At fifty-five years of age he maybe only had a couple of years to go before he hung up his raincoat and handed in his warrant card.

Moseley had no idea who his partner was. He was a younger guy. Mid-thirties. Bright eyed and bushy tailed. Much leaner and fitter than Randall. They were both wearing thigh length raincoats in a neat, casual style. Randall didn't look as imposing as he had in the past. Still at just one inch short of six feet tall he was still a decent size.

DCI Randall and his colleague approached Moseley. "What brings you here?" Randall asked.

"Long story," Moseley replied.

"Did you call it in?" asked the other cop.

"Yeah," Moseley replied.

"What's the score?" asked Randall in a less-than-thrilled manner.

"There's three men in the house. Two are tied up. The other is an imposter."

The cops soaked up the information, but didn't immediately reply. It was a few moments before Randall spoke. "An imposter of whom?" he asked.

"Ho Fung?"

"The businessman?" Randall asked.

"Yeah. Do you know him?" Moseley asked.

"I've seen him around."

"He's in my car recovering from an ordeal," said Moseley.

"Okay," said Randall and glanced up the street to the line of cars parked in the kerb. "Who are the guys in the house then?" he asked.

"No idea," said Moseley.

Several lights in the surroundings houses were coming on. Clearly the voices and the sight of a police car on the street had alerted some of the neighbours that there was police activity on the street.

"Can we get into the house?" Randall asked.

"Through the basement," Moseley replied.

"Let's go," said Randall. He paused for the briefest of moments. "This is my partner DI Tony Crocker." The younger detective nodded his head in Moseley's direction.

Both Randall and Crocker, followed by the two cops in uniform, made their way across the pavement. Moseley led them down the basement steps, along the corridor, up the steps and into the area by the lift door, then around the corner and into the vestibule.

Randall and Crocker took in the surroundings of the gold-leaf dragon statues and the bright colours of the old colonial Hong Kong flag in the glass frame attached to the wall.

"Where are the men you apprehended?" Randall asked.

"In a second-floor bedroom."

Randall looked at the two uniformed coppers. "One of you stay in here and guard the front door. If one of you comes with us, we'll see what we can find up here." He looked to Moseley. "You'd better lead the way," he requested.

Moseley led the way up the staircase to the first floor, along the landing, then up the second flight of stairs. He was followed closely by Randall and Crocker. A cop in uniform brought up the rear. His radio unit crackled and the alien sounding voice of a controller came over the air waves.

Just then the door of a room opened and a man who looked half asleep came onto the landing. He was dressed in a long silk robe that was hanging open over shiny deep crimson silk pyjamas. He rubbed sleep out of his eyes. It was the elderly man who had told Moseley he was Ho Fung.

Randall's eyes went to the man. He seemed to know him or recognise him. "You're Mr Ho Fung, aren't you?" he asked.

"Of course," said the chap. He took the sash attached to his robe and pulled it tight around his midriff. He looked aghast that people he didn't know were in the house.

Randall looked to Moseley. "I thought you said Mr Fung is in your car," he said.

"He is," Moseley snapped.

"But this is Mr Fung. I recognise him," said Randall.

"No, believe me he's in my car…" Moseley said.

"No. Believe me, this is Mr Fung," said Randall, leaving nothing to doubt.

"Are you sure?"

"Of course, I'm sure."

"How do you know him?" Moseley asked.

"He's a committee member of the British Hong Kong association. I attended one of their meetings in Mayfair about a year ago. I was introduced to Mr Fung at the event. This is him," said Randall.

Moseley looked stunned. "You're kidding, right?"

"No. I'm not kidding." Randall said in a curt tone.

It took a moment for the penny to drop through Moseley's head. When it dawned on him his jaw fell open. "If this is Mr Fung. Then who the fuck is sitting in my car?" he asked.

Randall shrugged his shoulders. "No idea," he replied.

"Oh, shit" Moseley immediately turned around, brushed past the uniformed cop and down the stairs as quickly as his legs could carry him. Randall was a few paces behind him. Once downstairs, Moseley went through the door and into the basement, down the steps and along the corridor. Randall caught up to him outside, but stopped at the top of the stairs leading onto the pavement.

Moseley scurried along the path at a brisk pace. Overhead there appeared to be the first crack of dawn light in the sky.

He was at his car within twenty seconds. He looked through the windscreen to see that the two people who, five minutes before, were sitting on the back seat were no longer there. They were nowhere to be seen. They had flown into the night. Literally disappeared into the dark. He couldn't do anything, but curse out loud. He was about to bang his fist on the bonnet when Randall caught up with him. He looked at Moseley.

"You've got some explaining to do," he said.

Moseley was too mortified to reply. He felt almost dumfounded and betrayed by his own sense of failure and lack of judgement. He put his hands to his head and just rested them on his forehead. DCI Randall asked him to accompany him back to number eighty-six.

By the time, they were back in the house, the two men who had been tied up were standing in the vestibule, alongside the two uniform cops, Crocker and the chap in the silk robe. The real Mr Fung. The smaller man had put on a pair of football shorts over his underwear. The stocky, heavy-built chap Moseley had grabbed by and ankles and pulled down the stairs was seething with anger, as well he might. Randall could see it might be about to turn nasty so he took Moseley by the arm and pulled him to a side. "Let's go into this room," he said. He beckoned to Crocker to accompany them into the reception room. The one with the fine baroque furniture, tiled fireplace, the large desk and the comfortable sofa. "You too Mr Fung. If that's okay with you, sir?"

Mr Fung nodded his head.

Once inside the room, Moseley went to the sofa and sat in the same seat he had occupied on his first visit to the house, to talk to the man who he now knew wasn't Ho Fung, but an imposter. The genuine Mr Fung sat in the black leather seat behind the mahogany desk. Randall and Crocker remained standing. The silver plate carriage clock atop of the mantel piece showed five minutes to three.

Randall looked to Moseley. "You'd better tell us all about it," he instructed.

Moseley sucked in a deep breath. "Where do I start?" he asked.

"How about at the start," suggested DI Crocker.

Moseley felt he was in for a long stretch. "Twelve days ago, I received a telephone call from a man who said he was Ho Fung. He asked me if I would go to Hong Kong to find his daughter-in-law – Lily Fung – and persuade her to return home. I requested that I meet him face-to-face. I came here in the afternoon of the same Monday and I was shown into this room by the woman who was in the second-floor room. I sat in this very seat. The man who said he was Ho Fung sat behind the desk."

"What did he ask you to do?" Randall asked.

"To go to Hong Kong. To visit the home of a man by the name of Leo Sinnott – the racehorse trainer – to ask him where she was."

"How did this fellow, the racehorse trainer know where she would be?" Randall asked.

"Because he was paid to entice her to Hong Kong."

"Why?"

"I don't know for sure."

"What happened then?"

"When I arrived in Hong Kong, I looked up an ex-cop called Laurie Sullivan."

"Where do you know him from?" asked Randall.

"I met him when I went to Hong Kong on an extradition case ten years ago. Sullivan showed me the sights and helped to find the assailant. We found Leo…"

"Who's the we?" Randall asked, cutting him off in mid-sentence.

"Sullivan and me."

"What did this Leo say?"

"He didn't deny any of it. Said Ho Fung had paid him to meet her in London. Get a love thing going then take her to Hong Kong. We asked him where she was. He said she was with him for two weeks, but she had left his pad without leaving a forwarding address. He hadn't seen her since. Both Sullivan and I asked him to take us to his apartment so we could check it out. He obliged. She wasn't there."

"What next?" asked Randall.

"It was a Wednesday night. Race night at Happy Valley so I went there to try and get Sinnott on my own."

"Why would you want to do that?" asked Crocker.

"I wanted to get him on my own, so I could ask him a few questions."

"Did you succeed?" Randall asked.

"Yeah. Sure."

"And?"

"And he didn't tell me a lot more. He confirmed he was paid to catch her eye and use his good looks and charm to persuade her to return to Hong Kong with him."

"So, they could form an everlasting relationship?" asked Crocker.

"Something like that," said Moseley.

Mr Fung was listening to the conversation in silence.

"Okay. So, you established that this guy was paid to entice this woman back to Hong Kong by someone who said he was Ho Fung."

Randall looked at the real Ho Fung. "Was that you Mr Fung?"

"No. Of course not," he retorted, as if such a thing was an absurd suggestion. "My son and daughter-in-law they live in Kensington."

"If it wasn't Mr Fung's daughter-in-law, then who is it?" Crocker asked.

"I've no idea," admitted Moseley.

"Okay. So, you speak to this guy who convinces you that the woman's gone. What happened next?" Randall asked.

"After I'd been to the racetrack to speak to Sinnott I returned to my hotel only to discover that my room had been broken into, but nothing was taken."

"Who did it?" Crocker asked.

"Not a clue. But it was obviously someone connected to all this."

"And?"

"The following day I meet with Laurie Sullivan in a bar in Wanchai. My drink was spiked and I passed out."

"Really?" said Crocker.

"Yeah. Really. I came around in a dark cell in God knows where. There was a bright white light shining into my eyes. Like something out of a spy movie. I couldn't see who was there. I was interrogated for a while, then I was injected with some drug. When I woke up two days later, I found myself in a wooden shack, laid on a mattress next to a dead body."

Both Randall and Crocker looked at each other. Randall blew out a shallow breath. "A body of whom?" he asked.

"The woman I had gone to Hong Kong to find."

"How did you know it was her?"

"Because of this photograph." Moseley reached into his jacket pocket and extracted the photograph the man who said he was Ho Fung had given him. He handed it to Randall.

Randall looked at it. He had a non-descript look on his face, but that changed after a few brief moments. His expression became one of puzzlement. "Oh, my word. Is it her?" he said to Crocker.

"Who?" Crocker asked.

Randall handed the photograph to his colleague. "Is it her?" Randall asked Crocker for a second time.

"Is it who?" Moseley asked.

"A missing woman called Lia Chung," replied Randall. Crocker examined the photograph. Randall finished the sentence. "She's been missing from her home in north London for three weeks."

"Who is Lia Chung?" asked Moseley. "And why haven't I heard about her?"

"She's a L.S.E academic and activist in the London branch of the Hong Kong pro-democracy movement. Her partner is a leading member of the movement. The reason why you haven't heard the name is because her family requested a news blackout in case they began receiving bogus ransom demands."

"Is her partner Lee Wang by any chance?" Moseley asked.

"Might be," said Randall.

Moseley sniffed. "He's the brother of Lily Fung. Is that right Mr Fung?"

"That is right," said Fung.

"How did this female die?" asked Crocker.

"There was drug paraphernalia all around the room," Moseley replied.

"Such as?" Randall asked.

"A white powdery substance. A syringe. Tinfoil. A spoon and a lighter. There was even a Bong for smoking something. It looked to me as if she may have died from a heroin overdose."

"Why would anyone want to kill her?" Randall asked.

"To send a message to those who would challenge the Hong Kong government," said Fung.

"What message is that?" DI Crocker asked.

"That the Hong Kong government has a long reach and can kill anyone who causes a problem. Or maybe they were trying to implicate Lee Wang."

"Do you know this Lee Wang?" asked Randall, looking at Ho Fung.

"Yes. He's been to my home on few occasion. I give him some money for the Free Hong Kong pro-independence movement."

Randall blew out another sigh as if to say this is heavy stuff for which he and his partner were not paid enough to get involved in. DI Crocker gave the photograph back to Randall. He took a couple of steps towards the desk. "Do you recognise them?" he asked and passed the photograph to Fung. He ran his eyes over it.

"Yes. That is Lia Chung with Lee Wang," he confirmed.

Randall bit his lower lip and rubbed a hand across his chin. It was latc. Hc was tircd. The synapses in his brain were finding it difficult to make all the necessary connections. If the truth be told so was Moseley.

Randall looked to Moseley. "So, after you woke up next to the dead body. What did you do then?" he asked.

"I managed to get out of the place and walk to a nearby town, from where I took a bus into Wanchai. I decided to pay Leo Sinnott a visit. I managed to sneak into the tower block and get onto his floor."

"Was he there?" DI Crocker asked.

"Yes, he was there."

"And?" Randall asked.

"He convinced me that he knew nothing about the death of the woman in the shack."

"Is that all?" asked Randall.

"He didn't believe me. He said he wanted to see the body."

"And you took him?" Randall asked.

"I took him to the place. When we got there everything had been removed. The body and all the evidence except for one item…"

"What was that?" Crocker asked, interrupting him in mid-flow

"They'd failed to remove a piece of curtain that was snagged on a nail."

"Is that all?"

"Yeah."

"What did this Sinnott do then?"

"Another man turned up. Between them they tried to silence me. He may have been one of the men who had interrogated me in the cell."

"When you say silence you. What do you mean?"

"Sinnott pulled a blade on me. A dagger of some type. He came at me."

"How did you get out of that?" Crocker asked as if he had serious doubts about the veracity of this whole story.

"I had to fight my way out. I stabbed Sinnott in the neck with a syringe…" Crocker put his hand to the base of his throat and rubbed his Adam's apple. "I managed to fight them off and escape. I got out and drove to Wanchai in Sinnott's car. Then I went to Kowloon and I was able to find Laurie Sullivan."

"What did he tell you?"

"Sullivan told me it was all about an attempt to discredit the pro-democracy movement."

"He told you *that*?" asked Randall.

"He couldn't very well attempt to wriggle out of it. I had him tied to a chair."

"Okay," said Randall.

Moseley glanced to the window where the dark of the night was still very much intact.

"What exactly was his role?" DI Crocker asked.

"Whose?" Moseley asked.

"Sullivan."

"To be brutally honest, I don't know for sure. I'm not sure of anything if the truth be told. I'm definitely not sure that anything he told me was true."

"What did he tell you?" Randall asked.

"Lots of things. Said it was an attempt to kill Lily Fung to discredit the British government at the same time. He said Lily Fung was involved in funding the pro-democracy movement. That the Hong Kong authorities were keen to stop her…."

"But it wasn't Lily Fung, was it? The person they wanted was Lia Chung," said Randall.

"So, it would seem. If that's her in the photograph," said Moseley.

"Why was Sullivan talking about Lily Fung?"

"I've no idea. Maybe that's what he was led to believe. He also said that Ho Fung is a spy for the Beijing government here in London with the task of monitoring and keeping tabs on Chinese dissidents."

"That is rubbish," said Fung raising his rasping voice for the first time.

Randall looked at Fung. "Who were the people in the house?"

Fung expressed an air of not understanding the question. "Which people?" he asked.

"The pair who were tied up?" Randall clarified.

"He is my personal assistant. Wan Jok and his wife. We long suspect that he was spying on me and working for the Hong Kong government. We suspect he was impersonating me to create confusion and spread misinformation among the Chinese community here in London."

"How long have you suspected them?" Randall asked.

"A few month," Fung replied.

"Why didn't you do anything about it?" Crocker asked.

"We not know for sure. It was only when he come here today…" Fung said looking at Moseley…" that we know for sure. We question him and he admits to everything."

"Admits to what?" Randall asked.

"That he was pretending to be me. He admit that he hire him…" he looked at Moseley again… "to go to Hong Kong to find Lia Chung, but they already know where she is."

"So, when Moseley came to the house to speak to you, he was actually speaking to your personal assistant. Wan Jok, who said he was you?" Randall asked.

"That correct."

"Where were you at the time of the visit?" Crocker asked.

"I in America visiting my daughter. She live there."

"So, your assistant had the house to himself?"

"That correct."

"What about your daughter-in-law. Lily."

"She live in Kensington with my son Hue."

"Is she involved in the pro-democracy movement?" Randall asked.

"Yes. We give a small amount of finance support."

"Where do you think Jok and his wife may have gone?" Crocker asked.

"I not know. They have help here in London."

"From whom."

"People in the Chinese community."

Randall sucked on his back teeth. He was perhaps considering the ramifications of this in diplomatic circles. After all, a British citizen – or at least one with dual British-Hong Kong citizenship had been enticed to go to Hong Kong to be murdered by elements attached to the Hong Kong administration. This could get very messy. He didn't want to go there or contemplate where it may end. He elected to say nothing for the moment.

"What was the racehorse trainer's role in all this?" DI Crocker asked to no one in particular.

"He a racehorse trainer, but I no longer have any horses with him. I sell my stake in a consortium called 'Ho Fung Belgravia Racing' a long time ago," said Fung.

"Why?"

"Because I discover that he work for Hong Kong government."

"What about Laurie Sullivan?" Crocker asked.

"I know Laurie Sullivan. He work for me in Hong Kong."

"Doing what?"

"Security task for my organisation. But he also work for Hong Kong government."

"How do you know?"

"People tell me."

Randall glanced at his watch, then he cleared his throat. "What I can gather is that both this racehorse trainer and Laurie Sullivan were working for the Hong Kong authorities, along with the guy who worked for Mr Fung. Mr Jok. Someone wanted to entice Lia Chung to Hong Kong so they used this trainer fellow."

"Is he some kind of stud?" Crocker asked.

Moseley answered the question. "Yeah. Something like that. In all seriousness he's a cool, good-looking guy with a reputation of a lady killer. He was rich, sophisticated and handsome. More than enough to turn any girl's head. I guess he was paid or told to contact her in London and persuade her to return to Hong Kong with him. She fell for him. She stayed with him for days, maybe a week or two. The man on the desk in the apartment building confirmed this."

"Confirmed what?" Crocker asked.

"That the woman in the photograph had stayed with Leo Sinnott in the apartment for some time, then she disappeared. If it was all a plot to kill her and implicate me then it very nearly came off."

"You talk of this guy in the past tense," said Crocker.

"Sinnott, might be dead," confessed Moseley.

"How?" Randall asked.

"I stabbed him in the neck with a syringe," said Moseley.

Neither Randall or Crocker chose to pursue this angle.

"Was it Sullivan who lead you to the racehorse trainer?" Randall asked.

"Yeah. The man I spoke to who now turns out to be this Jok fellow gave me the last known address of Lily Fung, who from what I am hearing now turns out to be Lia Chung. I knew Laurie Sullivan so decided to ask for his help. They must have known I would do that all along. When they were concocting the plot, they banked on me contacting Sullivan to tell him I …"

"Then they were right," said Randall cutting him off in mid-sentence. He looked at his watch and expressed surprise that the time was three-twenty. "May I suggest we wrap this up for now," he said. "I'll contact you tomorrow," he said addressing Ho Fung. "It seems to me as if this is now an issue for my superiors to see where they want to go with it. At the end of the day we may have discovered what happened to Lia Chung. If you're right…" he broke off to look at Moseley… "she could be dead. Let's leave it for now and I'll resume my investigations in the coming days. Are we in agreement?" he looked to Mr Fung. Fung didn't say a word but confirmed his agreement with a simple and almost prosaic nod of his head.

"Do you have any idea where Mr Jok and his wife could be?" Crocker asked Fung.

Fung shook his head. "They be on their way to China in the morning," he said with an air of inevitability in his tone.

"Okay. There's probably not a lot we can do until much later. We'll leave you in peace," said Randall.

With that Randall and Crocker led Moseley out of the room. The two uniformed cops were still standing by the front door. The thick set guy with the whiskers went into the reception room to consult with Ho Fung. The other guy in the t-shirt and shorts opened the front door and allowed the four cops and Moseley to leave by the most direct route.

Outside in the dark of the morning, the temperature was chilly. There was an edge to a northerly breeze wafting down the street. The first chink of light in the sky suggested dawn was two hours away. The thick, black painted door to number 86 Seaton Place was closed.

Moseley slipped his hands deep into the pockets of his jacket. He wondered if he would ever hear about this again. He surmised the British government would want to hush it up. No one wanted to create a rift in diplomatic circles or jeopardise the relationship between Britain and China. There was too much to lose. This entire episode might never see the light of day.

Moseley was going home to rest. He was convinced that tomorrow, or today as it now was, he wouldn't get much sleep. He would spend most of the day wondering what the hell happened to him in Hong Kong and why. The truth was he didn't know and perhaps he might never know the truth.

Chapter 20

Three days passed, Dave Moseley hadn't received any communication or correspondence from DCI Randall or anyone else in authority. He was starting to think he never would, but all that changed on Wednesday morning when he received a telephone call in his office.

He picked up the telephone, and introduced himself in the usual manner. "Dave Moseley Private Investigator. How can I help you today?" he said and waited for the caller's opening words. When they came, they were a little unusual to say the least.

The caller said: "My name is Roderick Smith from the Quaker Reform Fellowship Society." It was a middle-aged man's voice. He had a plummy Surrey accent.

"What can I do for you, Mr Smith?" Moseley asked.

"I'd like to invite you to a meeting of the society on Friday in a hotel close to Euston station," the man said.

Moseley assumed it was a crank call or a mistake. He was about to hang up on the caller, before something told him not to. He was intrigued if not a little confused. Perhaps he shouldn't have been. "I've never had any connection with the Quaker Society. Neither have I ever expressed any interest in joining such an institution," he said.

"Perhaps you should reconsider," said the caller.

"Why would I want to do that?"

"The society has postings all over the world."

"Like where?" Moseley asked.

"Hong Kong," replied the caller.

"Is that right?" Moseley said.

"It certainly is," replied Mr Smith. Moseley doubted it was his real name.

"So how can I assist you, Mr Smith?" he asked.

Mr Smith didn't reply for a long moment. "By attending the meeting," he said after the pause. "We need to meet with you to discuss your recent visit to Hong Kong. We need to know how you found the locals and what you learned about the place." His tone of voice had become more assertive and laced with subtle cadence and innuendo.

Moseley waited for a moment before replying. "I think in hindsight, I'd like to meet with you. Where and when do you want this to take place?"

"You'll receive some special delivery correspondence very shortly," said the caller. "The details of the location and the time of the meeting will be in the letter," he added.

"I look forward to receiving the letter," said Moseley. Before he could utter another word, the caller terminated the conversation. Moseley immediately pressed 1-4-7-1, but the message said the caller's number couldn't be traced.

He put the telephone down, sat back in his swivel chair and swung around one hundred and eight degrees to face the window with the view down to the street below. At ten-thirty, the activity on the street had reduced to little more than a thinly-spread number of people going about their business and few cars passing by. Sunlight was splintering through the edge of a cloud to splash a gold tipped wedge of light across the street and the rooftops of the building's opposite. The well-known coffee outlet on the corner was doing steady business. One and half hours before, during the morning rush hour, it was packed to the rafters.

He spun back to the desk, took the keyboard and typed 'Quaker Reform Fellowship Society' into the search engine and pressed the return button. A list of links popped up. The organisation or institution looked genuine enough. He assumed it was a front for another organisation, possibly one that was linked to a government agency. M.I something or other. Perhaps he was getting ahead of himself. Maybe it was an offshoot of the Serious Crime Unit based in New Scotland Yard.

As he replayed the conversation in his head there was a sound of someone pressing the button in the intercom at the front door downstairs. He got up from the desk, stepped out of the office and went down the stairs to the door at the bottom. At the door, he looked through a fish-eye spyhole to see a man dressed in the uniform of a Royal Mail postman, standing there with a manilla envelope in his hand. He had a peaked cap on his head with the common livery on it.

Nonetheless, Moseley was conscious of his own security and decided to stay on the alert. He made sure the thick metal safety chain was securely hooked into the locking device nailed into the door frame, then he opened the door to a narrow degree. When it was wide enough, he peered out through the gap and clapped his eyes on a skinny, short fellow with a pale face who was holding a A5 size envelope in his hand.

"Hello," he said to him.

"A special delivery letter for Mr David Moseley of Moseley Private Investigation," said the postman.

"That's me," Moseley said. "Slip it through the letter box, will you," he requested.

The man narrowed his eyes as if to say why can't you just open the door like anyone else? "You've got to sign for it. It's special delivery," he said. He dipped a hand into a jacket pocket and withdrew a pad and a pen.

"Pass them through the door," said Moseley.

"All right."

The postman slipped the envelope through the door. Moseley took it, then the chap threaded the pad and a cheap biro pen through the gap. Moseley took the pad. It looked authentic. He signed it against his name then handed it and the pen back to the postman, then promptly closed the door on him.

The envelope was marked with a 'Special Delivery' stamp. It was addressed to:

Mr David Moseley
46A Borthwick Street
Soho

London

SW3

He climbed the stairs back to his office, sat in the swivel chair behind the desk and ripped open the envelope. He extracted a piece of letter quality paper. It was headed: 'The Quakers' Reform Fellowship Society'

He read the content. It said:

Tuesday, 2nd May 2017

Dear Mr Moseley

We are delighted to invite you to attend the monthly meeting of the society, which will take place on Friday 5th May in the Lawton Hotel on Grafton Way, Euston Road. NW1 3BT.

Please arrive for a prompt start at 12 noon. The meeting will last for one hour.

Tea and Coffee will be available at the meeting.
We very much look forward to meeting you on the day.

Yours sincerely

Roderick Smith

Society Chairperson.

It was signed by Mr Smith. At the bottom was a long number and a reference to a charity. How very cloak and dagger, thought Moseley. A simple telephone call could have done that or an email, but both those forms of communication could be easily traced, whereas the Royal Mail can easily lose a signature.

He had never been to the Lowton Hotel so he looked it up on-line. He discovered it was a small hotel, mainly catering for budget travellers and those wanting to be close to Euston, St Pancras or Kings Cross railway stations.

It would be interesting to discover what transpired at the meeting. He was in no doubt that it was either an information gleaning exercise or perhaps a diplomatic service, organised event.

Chapter 21

Friday began overcast and cool. As the morning progressed towards noon the clouds cleared and the temperature went up a couple of notches. The traffic on Euston Road was nose to tail. That was nothing unusual. As a major link road, serving routes into both north and east London, Euston Road was always busy. Moseley knew the vicinity well having worked in nearby Bloomsbury when he was first drafted into the Mets detective core.

He was dressed in a dark lounge suit, blue shirt and blue tie. He was carrying the black leather document holder which contained the report he had written for Ho Fung. The one he had never been able to give to the client, as he had vanished into the night. He was still very much reflecting on his negligence and the haste which had caused him to be less than professional when he took the job. It was a lesson he had learned the hard way.

Since receiving the telephone call on Wednesday and the letter, he had been wondering who the Quaker society were. He would soon find the answer to the question. He slipped down the street off Euston Road in the area close to the entrance to Regents Park and made his way along Grafton Street. The Lowton Hotel was just ahead. The time by his watch said two minutes to twelve. He turned off the path, through the entrance and into the hotel reception area. It was nothing special. Not very inspiring at all. It was a small hotel. No more than twenty rooms at a guess, catering for transient business travellers and those on a moderate budget.

He stepped close to a tightly hemmed-in counter where there was an unmanned desk, that held a computer and telephone. A replica grandfather clock chimed twelve noon.

Then he saw the display board attached to the wall by the side of a corridor. A notice said: 'The Quakers Reform Fellowship Society' in the 'Tavistock meeting room'. A pointed finger sign signalled the way down the corridor.

As there was no one close by he stepped down the corridor, found a door marked: The 'Tavistock' and tapped on it.

Within a couple of seconds, the door opened and a man who looked remarkably like the postman who had handed him the envelope appeared. This time he wasn't wearing a postman uniform, but a worsted jacket, and matching trousers. The jacket had a pin badge in the lapel. He looked far more debonair in the jacket, shirt and tie, than he had in the postman's garb. He wasn't a big man by any stretch of the imagination. He eyed Moseley for a moment. "Come in," he said and opened the door wide.

Moseley stepped into a relatively cramped meeting room which was dominated by a large rectangular, walnut topped table at which two men were sitting in stout chairs, down the left side. A lady of about forty or thereabouts was at the top of the table. Everyone was dressed in smart-casual officc attirc. Thc lady was sitting with her back to a pair of French windows that opened onto a small garden. She was in a frumpy looking dress and matching cardigan. The natural light pouring into the room through the door was enough to brighten the setting, though the bulb in a round glass shade attached to the ceiling was on. A hostess type trolley along one side held a tea and coffee machine, plus cups and saucers, and individual packets of custard cream biscuits.

The man who had opened the door went to take a third seat next to his colleagues. "Please be seated," he said to Moseley, gesturing to the right side of the table.

Moseley sat down in the first chair. He made eye contact with the two men and they exchanged nods of the head. It was a few moments before the man opposite him began to talk. He introduced himself in rather a bumptious manner.

"Mr Moseley. My name is Anthony Wordsworth and I'm the society president and chairman of this meeting." He was a tall, thin guy in his mid-forties. He spoke with a home counties accent. No doubt public school educated.

"This is my colleague Mr Raymond Smalley." He was an equally well turned out, balding chap, older than the chairman and had the look of a university professor or academic. He was unsmiling but not as serious looking as the chairman. A pair of wire-framed, thick lens spectacles covered his eyes. He looked as if he had been ordered to attend a meeting he didn't want to be at.

"And this is Miss Stannard. She is the society secretary and will be taking minutes of this meeting."

She cracked a half-smile at Moseley. She was a dowdy looking woman with shoulder length auburn hair. She didn't go heavy on make-up. "You've met Mr Smith before."

"Anyone for tea or coffee?" Miss Stannard asked.

Mr Wordsworth requested a tea. Mr Smalley asked for a black coffee with no sugar. Mr Smith didn't want a drink. Moseley also declined the offer of a hot beverage. He got the impression it was all stage managed and orchestrated. He had few doubts that they were Security Services aligned to MI5 or more likely they were Foreign Office personnel. Definitely not police. They were not coarse enough for bobbies.

Miss Stannard went to the tea and coffee machine and prepared the drinks for the men. Moseley had to smile to himself. He now knew for certain that these were Foreign Office people. The lady in the party was expected to make the men their beverages. Sexual equality hadn't quite reached organisations like this. They were still behind the modern times.

Once he had a cup of tea, Mr Wordsworth looked at Moseley, but waited for Miss Stannard to be seated before getting underway. She sat down, took a pen out of her handbag and placed it down on a thick pad of paper in front of her.

Wordsworth began. "Mr Moseley, I understand that you recently undertook an assignment in Hong Kong. Would you like to tell us about it? I understand you went there to try to locate a missing person." His accent was very similar to Mr Smith's. The aroma of the hot coffee made Moseley wish he ought to have accepted the offer of a drink.

He pursed his lips. "Perhaps you wouldn't mind telling me just who you are?" he said.

"Why? We're the Society of Quakers," said Mr Smith. Miss Stannard wrote something onto the pad of paper.

"Yeah. And I'm…" he was going to say something witty but went off the idea. It would attract zero laughs. He decided in that moment to play ball.

"Perhaps you may like to start by telling us exactly how you were made aware of a missing person," said Smith.

"Fine. I received a telephone call from a man purporting to be Ho Fung. He asked me to go to Hong Kong to find his missing daughter-in-law. That was his brief. Plain and simple."

"When was this?" Wordsworth asked.

"The telephone call and subsequent meeting were three weeks this coming Monday."

"When did you leave?"

"The day after."

"Where did you stay?"

"At a hotel in Wanchai."

"What was the name of the hotel?"

"The Wanchai Mandarin Garden."

"When you set out to find the missing woman who did you contact first?"

"A guy by the name of Laurie Sullivan."

"What was your connection to him?"

"I knew him from the time I went out there to extradite a wanted criminal back to these shores." Miss Stannard wrote the name on her pad.

"What did Mr Sullivan advise?"

"That I contact someone called Leo Sinnott."

"Can you spell that?" asked Miss Stannard.

"L-E-O S-I-N-N-O-T-T."

"Who is he?" Smith asked.

"He was the name of a person I was given by a chap who said he was Mr Fung."

"Why?" asked Mr Smith.

"He told me Sinnott had taken his daughter-in-law to Hong Kong and he might know of her whereabouts."

"What does this chap do?" asked Mr Smalley.

"Do? For a job?"

"Yes."

"He's a racehorse trainer at Happy Valley racetrack."

"And what is his connection to all this?"

"He's a kind of stud I'd guess you'd say," Moseley said. He wasn't in any way embarrassed to use such a term in the presence of the woman. She didn't bat an eyelid. "I suppose you could say he put it about a bit. According to Mr Fung he had whisked Lily Fung to Hong Kong on a romantic quest, but in reality, it was a scheme to get her back to Hong Kong for other reasons.

"But she wasn't Lily Fung. She was Lia Chung. Is that right?" asked Smith.

"Yes. From what I now understand. When I was first shown a photograph by a man pretending to be Mr Fung, I was told it was Lily Fung, not Lia Chung."

“And he wasn’t the real Ho Fung. Was he?”

“That would also appear to be the case,” said Moseley picking his words carefully.

“Thank you,” said Smith. “Perhaps you would like to tell us in your own words the full story from the word go.”

“Let me do that.”

Miss Stannard turned over a fresh sheet of paper. Moseley obliged them. He told them the full story from the very top. He effectively told them the full account in a statement spanning five segments. He told them of how he was first approached by the bogus Ho Fung to the moment he felt dizzy in the ‘Old Country’ pub. Then from the time he woke up in the cell to the moment he woke up on the bed next to the naked dead body of the person he believed to be Lily Fung. Then how he managed to get out of the shack and make it back into Leighton Hill to find Leo Sinnott. How he stabbed him in the neck with the syringe and so forth. The fourth segment began when he went into Kowloon to find Laurie Sullivan. Tied him to the chair with the beads of the door curtain and how he whacked him in the face with the base of the pan. The fifth and final instalment covered the events of last Sunday morning in Belgravia.

When he had completed telling them the account, those in the room could only reflect on what he had told them. They then asked him a series of questions which he answered to the best of his ability and truthfully. They seemed satisfied that he had furnished them with a true account of what had happened.

The meeting lasted for five minutes short of one hour, then he was invited to leave. They never told him who they were. He suspected they were Foreign Office personnel who were assigned to investigate the Lia Chung case.

He doubted that he would ever hear from them again, but he couldn't be sure.

It was just a few minutes before one when Moseley left the hotel. As he stepped out onto the street, he looked at the brightening sky and felt a warm edge to the breeze, but he still shuddered his shoulders, sunk his hands into the deep recess of his jacket pockets and made a fist of his hands. It wasn't cold. It was just a trait of his.

He would have loved to have been a fly on the wall in the meeting room, listening to what those people were discussing. If they were Foreign Office personnel, as he assumed, they would have a tricky balancing act to perform. A crime had taken place in the jurisdiction of a rising political and military power. He doubted if the British government would want to make many waves when it came to dealing with the aftermath. The amount of trade Britain did with both the Hong Kong authorities and the Chinese - not to mention the inward investment – were far too important to be derailed by the death of a British citizen who also held Hong Kong citizenship. What they reported to their superiors and what they recommended would determine the course of action they would take. Moseley doubted those at the top would want to take it much further.

That is exactly how it turned out. Eight days after the meeting in the Lowton Hotel, the story broke in the mainstream news media of how the body of the twenty-nine-year-old missing L.S.E lecturer – called Lia Chung – had been found washed up in a rocky cove close to a remote beach on the south side of Hong Kong island. Apparently, the theory was that she had gone for a late-night swim in a bay close to a beach resort. She must have got into difficulties because of the strong currents that took her out of the shallow water. Her body was found trapped under rocks then washed up on the shore. Hence the delay in finding her. The official cause of death was drowning by misadventure.

Within a day of the announcement, Moseley received a telephone call from Roderick Smith from the 'Quaker Reform Fellowship Society'. He made Moseley an offer he couldn't refuse. Smith told him that he would receive a cheque from the society for the sum of £15,000 if he signed a confidentiality agreement. The agreement was that he would never tell anyone about his assignment in Hong Kong. Moseley agreed.

It was all over. He would never receive another telephone call or another request from the 'Quaker Reform Fellowship Society'. He never did discover if Leo Sinnott and Laurie Sullivan had survived. Perhaps they were alive. Perhaps they were eliminated by their masters for their failure to kill Moseley and failure to put him in the frame for the death of Lia Chung. He never did discover if the authorities had managed to apprehended Wan Jok and his wife. He thought there were two chances of finding them: slim and none.

He wanted to forget all about it. To be honest, he decided, missing person tasks were off his to-do list for some considerable time to come. He could do without them. They were far too dangerous.

The End

About the author….

Neal Hardin lives in Hull, England. He is the author of several novels, novellas and short stories. His first published novel, 'The Go-To Guy' was published in March 2018, by Stairwell Books, based in York, England; and Norwalk, Connecticut, USA.

Before retiring in 2016, Neal worked in the Education sector for over 21 years. He enjoys travelling whenever possible. He has visited the United States and Canada on many occasions, along with Japan, China, Australia and other countries. He follows his local football team and enjoys most sports and working out in the gym. He continues to write and enjoys the discipline of writing and constructing great stories.

Neal Hardin is also the author of…

Dallas After Dark
A Gangland Tale
The Four Fables
Moscow Calling
On the Edge
The Wish-List
A Titanic Story
The Taking of Flight 98
Perilous Traffic
Triple Intrigue
Soho Retro

All these novels are available to purchase on Amazon

See me on Twitter @HardinNealp

Printed in Great Britain
by Amazon

62450316R00130